"I'm more interested in what killed him," Detective Murray said, squatting down again to look the victim in the eye. "That's some serious shit, Hall."

She started taking notes and looking for interesting clues. "How's that, Henderson?" she asked, not really listening.

"You ever kill a chicken, Eleanora?" he looked back over a shoulder at her.

"I'm from Juanita, you silly-ass redneck," she made a face at him. "Would have ruined my nails."

"So, to do the job, you grab a chicken by the head and pull really hard, El," he said. "Comes right off. Heart still pumps for a bit, so you get blood everywhere. Kinda like this."

"So you're telling me," she said with heavy irony, "that somebody ripped his head off? How?"

Murray shrugged. "I have no idea. Couldn't have been a person," he said. "Nobody's that strong."

Hall shrugged back at him. She knew better than to ask where he came up with some of his crazier ideas. "Well, at least the murderer cleaned up the streets a little, killing this piece of shit," she said. "Now if we can just get enough rain to wash it all off."

Imposters
Blaze Ward
Copyright © 2015 Blaze Ward
All rights reserved
Published by Knotted Road Press
www.KnottedRoadPress.com

ISBN: 978-0692444245

Cover art:
© Rolffimages | Dreamstime.com - Eyes Photo

Cover and interior design copyright © 2015 Knotted Road Press

Never miss a release!
If you'd like to be notified of new releases, sign up for my newsletter.

I only send out newsletters once a quarter, will never spam you, or use your email for nefarious purposes. You can also unsubscribe at any time.

http://www.blazeward.com/newsletter/

Imposters

BLAZE WARD

Knotted Road Press
www.KnottedRoadPress.com

Also by Blaze Ward

Auberon: The Jessica Keller Chronicles Volume 1

Collections
Beyond the Mirror: Volume 1 Fantastic Worlds
Beyond the Mirror: Volume 2 Fantastic Worlds
Beyond the Mirror: Volume 3 Alternate Worlds

Rick Pine Stories
The Shipwrecked Mermaid
Imposters

Science Fiction Stories
The Earthquake Gun
Greater Than The Gods Intended
The Librarian
Moscow Gold
Myrmidons

Javier Aritza Stories
The Science Officer
The Mind Field

Brak Stories
Destiny
The Meat Shield
The Popcorn Kitten

Zolnerovy Stories
Valeryia
Tatiyana

Imposters

BLAZE WARD

Prologue

Detective Eleanora Hall climbed out of the passenger side of the sedan and looked down the long alley.

A typical Seattle rain fell, just enough to wash away most of the evidence, not enough to actually clean anything up. Great waste of a Friday night. Story of her life.

She pulled up her hood and made sure her badge was visible outside her rain shell, on a cute little necklace her husband had bought her, as she made her way through the small crowd that had gathered on the street.

"What have you got, Kowolski?" Detective Hall said as she stepped up to the police tape the enterprising officer had already hung across the alleyway.

The officer nodded to her and pointed back behind him. "Got a bad one, ma'am," he said. He glanced at his watch. "Shop keeper found him about twenty minutes ago, already cold. Called. I was a few blocks away. Took a look. Haven't done much but block it off and call for help."

Detective Hall felt her partner come up beside her. Detective Henderson Murray was as old school as the department got. She watched him light a cigarette and take a drag as he listened. He liked to listen a lot. Didn't speak until he had mulled it all over for a while. People liked to talk. They usually said too much around him.

She nodded at the officer. "So time of death prior to 2AM?" She waited for him to nod back before she slid under the tape.

It was a good thing she was wearing her practical boots tonight instead of something more dressy. Blood splattered on the walls, the dumpster, the concrete. It dripped from the rain and ran in the gutter.

It was going to be one of those nights.

"That's one from the history books," Detective Murray said with an intrigued voice.

The victim was even worse than the reports had suggested. The body was in at least three major pieces.

"What's your take, Murray?" Detective Hall asked her partner as he squatted down and poked at *something* with a pen. He was Murray. Never Henderson, or Hend, or anything. Just Murray.

She watched him work for a moment. "Somebody, *something*, literally tore this poor bastard to pieces," he said, standing. "That's a leg. The other one's over there and, wow…"

Detective Hall followed Detective Murray as he stood and stepped around the dumpster. Whatever it was that had killed the man had decapitated him afterwards and carefully jammed his head onto a rusty iron bar wedged into a manhole cover.

"So much for Pookie," she said to herself.

"Know the guy?" Murray asked.

The neck was torn like a piece of newspaper, rather than chopped cleanly like a knife would do. The head had belonged a young black man.

"Yeah," she replied. "Small time punk. Occasional dealer, part-time pimp, guaranteed to snitch when we caught him. Used to run into him when I worked Central District and Rainier Beach. Wonder what brought him up to Belltown?"

"I'm more interested in what killed him," Detective Murray said, squatting down again to look Pookie in the eye. "That's some serious shit, Hall."

She started taking notes and looking for interesting clues. "How's that, Henderson?" she asked, not really listening.

"You ever kill a chicken, Eleanora?" he looked back over a shoulder at her.

"I'm from Juanita, you silly-ass redneck," she made a face at him. "Would have ruined my nails."

"So, to do the job, you grab a chicken by the head and pull really hard, El," he said. "Comes right off. Heart still pumps for a bit, so you get blood everywhere. Kinda like this."

"So you're telling me," she said with heavy irony, "that somebody ripped his head off? How?"

Murray shrugged. "I have no idea. Couldn't have been a person," he said. "Nobody's that strong."

Hall shrugged back at him. She knew better than to ask where he came up with some of his crazier ideas. "Well, at least he cleaned up the streets a little, killing this piece of shit," she said. "Now if we can just get enough rain to wash it all off."

Chapter 1

Rick sat at the petite little bar at the front of his bistro and considered his need for a cigarette.

They wouldn't let you smoke indoors anymore in Washington state. And outside it was that kind of heavy, misty, dewy Seattle rain that was just past annoying, but not quite serious. He couldn't decide if he really wanted to go stand out in it for a nicotine fix, or just sit there at the bar and nurse a small glass of red wine.

Rick glanced at his image in the bar back mirror, saw a tall, kinda-skinny white guy. Thirty-one hard years. Splattered chef jacket unbuttoned. Faded blue jeans.

Technically, it was his bar, since he was a half owner of the joint, but he spent almost all of his time in the kitchen cooking when he was here. So, really it was Her bar. She was, after all, the one who spent almost all her time at it.

He turned to watch Bethany looking down at him, a sardonic arch to one gorgeous eyebrow that conveyed more emotion, humor, and information than he could probably manage with a ten minute head start and a triple shot of espresso.

He smiled back at her. She was easy to look at. Tall. Taller than his six foot one if she wore any kind of heels. Smooth skin the color of chocolate milk.

Beautiful in a way that Greek sculptors would have preserved in granite. A smile that could warm an entire room.

Amazingly well-preserved for a woman in her early fifties, too. Had apparently been a model when she was younger. You could tell. Looked thirty-five. Maybe. Technically old enough to be his mother, but that probably wouldn't have stopped him with any other woman.

But not her. Absolutely not a person to be trifled with, under any circumstances. Total shark. Smart as a whip, too, which was good, because he really didn't know anything about the business side of running a bistro. That was why her little brother, Gustav, Deputy Harcourt who had been his jailer and guardian angel in prison, had helped pair him up with her when he had gotten out of prison eight months ago.

All Rick had wanted to do was cook. Sure, exotic things, this was Ballard, after all, but having a partner like her meant he could just have fun back there. Or, like now, just drink a glass of red wine to unwind from a long day.

Sundays were always hell. The end of a long week, including getting up early to do weekend brunch twice. But now, forty hours of down-time, until Tuesday dinner.

Laundry. Groceries. Sleep. Maybe smoke a whole pack of cigarettes, just because he could.

"Penny for your thoughts, Rick," Bethany said with a soft smile.

God, even her voice was sexy. She knew it, too. He really needed to get out and find a girlfriend or something. Eight years incarcerated. Eight months of working himself into utter exhaustion pretty much daily. And God pairs him with the hottest woman in Ballard as a business partner.

Rick took a large drink of the wine in his glass.

"Ask me again Tuesday," he said finally, "after about twelve hours of sleep. Right now, not sure they're worth that much."

She started to say something to that. Knowing her, something caustic and hilarious and ever-so-slightly off-color, that would have him rolling on the carpet, gasping for air.

He needed to find a woman like that that he didn't own a bistro with.

The little bell attached to the front door interrupted her. For a moment, the sounds of 22nd Avenue. Traffic on Market in the distance.

He felt Bethany's attention turn away from him and towards the door. It was like the room got colder. Probably better that way.

"Good evening," she said, that warm alto voice filling the otherwise quiet joint. "The kitchen is closed for the evening, but the bar is open for wine or espresso. What can I get started for you?"

"A sixteen ounce caramel mocha, please."

Something about the voice made Rick look into the mirror to see its owner. Something just didn't sound right.

For one, it didn't sound like a five-foot-two Japanese-American woman. And she was. Long black hair pulled back and tied. Great big green eyes. Perfect skin. Wicked little smile on her face.

She made eye contact with him in the mirror and took a step in his direction. "Are you Rick?"

His mind placed the nearest bottle of wine, in case he needed to have a club suddenly. He got cold all over and a surge of adrenalin hit his empty stomach.

Eight years in prison will do that to you.

But in addition to that, her voice just didn't sound right. The scenario wasn't right. This wasn't some porno, where a beautiful woman walked into a bar, fell in love with you at first sight, and threw herself at you as the music started grinding up.

And it sure felt that way.

Rick tensed, unconsciously, spiking her eyes in the mirror. He nodded, unwilling to say anything at this point that might betray him more.

She smiled back and took two small steps forward to slide onto the stool nearest the front window. Suddenly she was almost within touching range.

Rick got a good look at her as she did. Skin-tight black jeans tucked into twenty-ring Doc Martens. Bright green t-shirt under a black leather jacket, half-zipped against the weather.

He watched her set a small messenger bag, not a purse, on her lap and flip it open. One of his hands twitched, nearly reaching for the pepper mill. The big, heavy, wooden, club-shaped pepper mill.

Okay. Maybe he hadn't left his past as far behind as he'd thought.

The girl seemed to sense his uneasiness. She smiled up at him as she flipped the bag open. "So a while back," she said with a light smile, "you did a huge favor for a friend of mine. And she borrowed something from you at the time. She asked me to return it. Took forever to find you."

She? Rick got a puzzled-dog look on his face. He'd been in prison for a very long time, and since he got out, the only women he'd been around had been Bethany and Gwen, the bistro's primary waitress. Past that, the only other woman he could think of was…

Oh.

Shit.

Rick knew without looking in the mirror that his eyes were about the size of saucers right now. He tried to remember to breathe. His mind went numb. He *really* needed that cigarette right about now.

The little *Sansei* girl smiled at him. It was a warm smile. It was still a shark smiling.

He watched her reach into the messenger bag and pull out a black cotton bundle. "Well, two things, actually," she said.

She pulled the cloth back to reveal a battered, stainless steel travel mug, printed with the world's biggest coffee shop on the side, in the middle of a Queen of Hearts from a card deck.

His mug.

The last time he had seen it had been a year ago. *In the hands of a... Ah, hell, in the hands of a mermaid, like the logo on the mug, right before her spaceship took off.*

An alien mermaid.

He and Gustav had stood on the shore, right before sunrise, and watched her spaceship fly away. Climb out of the water, level off, look at them, and then shoot into the sky impossibly fast.

Rick watched this little imposter set the mug on the bar in front of him. Who knew what interstellar adventures his mug had just come back from.

She flattened the black cotton bundle out to reveal an old faded t-shirt printed with the name of a band he had been into, back before, before prison.

"I've never heard of these guys," she said.

"They broke up about a decade ago," he responded automatically. He still had two CD's they had cut in a garage studio, once upon a time.

Rick's brain finally caught up to his pounding heart. "I'm surprised she didn't keep the shirt."

"She had it copied," the girl smiled mischievously at him. "Wears it constantly."

Shit.

Bethany slipped a white porcelain saucer onto the bar and sat a cup of steaming mocha down.

"Rick," she said with a knowing smile, "I'll be in back doing paperwork. Yell if you need help."

He watched her give the new girl a smile, almost a knowing look and a smile as she moved towards the back. God, it felt like that time his mom had caught him and Tina necking on the sofa. Rick could feel himself blushing.

Fine. Whatever.

Rick sat his wine down and held out a hand. "Hi, I'm Rick."

She took his hand in a dry handshake. That didn't feel right either, but that was probably him at this point.

"Laurie Bradley," she said. "Nice to finally meet you, Rick. Heard a lot about you."

Rick swallowed down a throat that threatened to strangle itself. "What can I do for you, Laurie?"

Her face got serious. "We need your help."

Yup. That was exactly how it started last time.

Bethany looked out over the bar and considered the bistro.

Her bistro.

Sure, she had a partner, but he lived in back and made the most wonderful food. It was her charm, her connections, her savvy that had gotten them this far. Now, it was up to Rick and his fabulous cooking to carry them the rest of the way. To make this place *big*.

She found it hard to imagine that it had been just over a year now. Last September, when her little brother Gustav, and Daniel's daughter Eloise, her niece, had come to her and told her it was time to get over herself.

Bethany glanced at the calendar on the wall and quickly did the math. Four years and three months since Charles had died. Time to, not move on, but start living again. Time to get back to work and stop moping around the house. She hadn't needed the money. Charles had seen to that. Ever prepared, that man.

No, what she had needed was a challenge, a widow at fifty-two whose only daughter lived in Boston these days. So how did she feel about becoming a partner in a bistro? Oh, and, your partner will be a young man who just did eight years for armed robbery.

Bethany smiled. Those had been lovely arguments. Her little brother Gustav was almost as stubborn as she was. And their niece apparently got the requisite hard head that ran in the family.

And now, here she was. Her bar. Her place. Their bistro.

Bethany smiled to herself as she looked over the quaintness of it all. She expanded it to include Rick as she looked down at him, exhaustion carved into his face. He worked harder than any cook she had known, at any of the restaurants she had owned over the years.

That boy had something to prove, but not to her.

She wasn't sure she should even ask. Rick had some personal demons, she had seen that, but he had never been anything but a perfect gentleman around her.

Oh, he watched her, when he thought she wasn't looking, the way a man watches a woman walk. But she knew she intimidated the hell out of him.

Still...

"Penny for your thoughts, Rick," she said, smiling warmly at him as his sipped a glass of red.

"Ask me again Tuesday," Rick replied, tiredness evident in the rough gravel of his voice, "after about twelve hours of sleep. Right now, not sure they're worth that much."

She thought about teasing him some. They were alone. He could relax. She might even let her hair down a little.

The little brass bell on the door interrupted her.

A customer walked in, damp from the rain.

"Good evening," Bethany said to her, taking her measure. The newcomer was petite, coming up to Bethany's chin, perhaps, and Asian. She was dressed casual. Jeans, heavy boots, leather jacket, messenger bag slung over a shoulder.

"The kitchen is closed for the evening, but the bar is open for wine or espresso. What can I get started for you?"

The woman glanced once around the bar, settled her eyes on Rick, and smiled a little smile to herself.

"A sixteen ounce caramel mocha, please."

Bethany watched the girl home in on her partner. "Are you Rick?"

She considered Rick's reaction. Obviously he didn't know her. He became cold and reserved. It was like a light switch was flipped off. *Interesting.*

Bethany pulled hardware and started to brew, keeping a sharp eye on the stranger as the little girl sat at the bar. Rick could take care of himself. That, she knew from Gustav.

"So a while back," Bethany heard the girl begin, "you did a huge favor for a friend of mine. And she borrowed something from you at the time. She asked me to return it. Took forever to find you."

Bethany brewed the mocha automatically as her focus stayed on the Asian woman. She watched the messenger bag come forward and flip open. Rick got nervous, but stayed perfectly still.

Mad ex-girlfriend thing? After this long? Probably not.

The girl pulled out a wadded up t-shirt wrapped around something. She unrolled it to reveal a banged-up steel coffee mug. Rick blinked.

"Well, two things, actually," Bethany heard her say.

The T-shirt was a band she knew Rick occasionally listened to, back in the kitchen, while he was prepping. Lord knows she preferred good jazz to bad punk.

"I've never heard of these guys," the stranger said.

Rick's eyes were focused on the shirt. *Curious.*

"They broke up about a decade ago," Bethany heard him reply. "I'm surprised she didn't keep the shirt."

"She had it copied," Laurie replied. "Wears it constantly."

Bethany smiled to herself.

Oh ho. So it was an ex-girlfriend. And this was a friend of hers who had apparently decided it was finally safe to chase after the boy. Not that she had ever done that, right? Poor Jill had let Charles get away, after all. Bethany just hadn't let him get very far.

Ah, young love.

Bethany's hands finished the drink automatically and styled a fern leaf into the cream.

She set it on the bar and took a moment to study this new girl closely. After so long in prison, Rick wouldn't be thinking clearly, especially not if some hot little chickie came along and started batting her pretty little eyelashes at him.

Bethany would just have to be Momma Hen and keep him safe.

"Rick," she said, putting them both on notice, in spite of her warm, friendly tones, "I'll be in back doing paperwork. Yell if you need help."

Bethany watched Rick blush and the girl blink at her.

Good. Message delivered.

She sashayed back to the little office and sat down. It had a mirror positioned to watch the front of the bistro, so she could keep an eye on the two of them. From what she could see, it was an interesting conversation. A little more serious than she expected. The girl wasn't flirting all that much, but her body language was centered entirely on Rick. Must have been a hell of a breakup, once upon a time.

After a few minutes, Rick slid backwards off the stool, stripped off his chef coat, and grabbed his rain shell off the coat hook just beside the bar.

"Bethany," he called, "I'm going to head out with Laurie. Kitchen is clean. Can you lock up?"

Laurie, huh? Interesting. This ought to make for an stimulating conversation when she saw him again Tuesday.

Bethany regretted now that they were closed on Mondays and didn't open for lunch on Tuesdays. That was an awful lot of time for him to get into trouble. Still, he was a big boy. He could handle himself.

"Absolutely, Rick," she called back. "You two have fun."

She smiled as they went out the door. Maybe a girlfriend was just what he needed.

Larek considered the door of the small restaurant. No, damn it. *Laurie.* She had to keep focused on that part. Larek was a part of her that was gone now, maybe forever. She was Laurie. Focusing on the name would remind her to be human when she forgot.

The sign on the bistro's door said *Flotsam.* She pulled out her cute little human smart-phone and looked up the term. There were several definitions available in English. The most poetical was *Things cast ashore after a storm.* Considering one of the owners, she wondered how much of that was an inside joke on the world.

Larek, *Laurie,* approached the glass door and took a second to check her image in the reflection, this strange alien creature.

She looked human enough to pass, woman enough to have been propositioned more than once today, although Intelligence on human males suggested they were often less than discriminating. Still, the re-design was working very well.

Learning to dance again after they upgraded her "breasts" to something heavier and more prominent from the original design had been the hardest part. Still, she had learned that human men, the dominant gender on this planet, tended to make eye contact a lot less since her chest had become more impressive. And they concentrated far less on any verbal gaffes she made.

Every little bit to make the disguise better.

She opened the door.

As restaurants went, it was small, almost tiny, more like what she would have expected in a dive downtown than a semi-suburb like Ballard. Still, it had a quaint charm she found inviting.

Six tables down the wall on her left, two larger ones on the ends with four smaller ones in the middle. A back wall that probably marked the rest room. Kitchen, office, and storage on the right in back. A small bar on the immediate right, with dozens of wine bottles and an espresso machine behind. Three stools in front of it.

Behind a bar, an amazingly-tall African-American woman, beautiful by standards well beyond just human, smiled at her.

"Good evening," the woman said quietly. According to the intelligence report, she was one of the two owners. Not the one she was here to see. "The kitchen is closed for the evening, but the bar is open for wine or espresso. What can I get started for you?"

Laurie considered all the options available in a modern Bistro fashioned on the French model. Her newly-upgraded liver could handle wine better than any human's could, requiring perhaps an entire bottle to notice any sensory alterations. Still, there was one human thing she really craved right now.

"A sixteen ounce caramel mocha, please," she replied.

Sitting at the bar was her target. Rick Pine. Human male. Age 31. Former criminal convict, a "felon," who nonetheless scored top numbers in reliability and trustworthiness. Six foot, one inch tall, two hundred ten pounds. Dark brown hair that needed to be cut. A nose that had been broken once and not quite reset properly.

When Larek had been rebuilt as the human Laurie, she had also been reprogrammed to react to many things in a human, a female, manner. Laurie found Rick attractive in a rough, unfinished kind of way.

Larek would have been aghast, considering all that body hair and strange dimensions, but Larek was the past. She needed to embrace the human.

Laurie took a step closer and smiled at him. He appeared to be nervous.

"Are you Rick?" she asked.

When he nodded at her, she closed the short distance and sat on the third stool, close to him, but leaving a chair between. Unconsciously, he flinched, so Laurie decided she needed to charm him, to *flirt* in the human manner. She smiled.

Laurie reached behind her and pulled her satchel onto her lap. Inside, she found the bundle she had been entrusted with by, the mermaid scout, Amaleti, back at base.

"So a while back," Laurie said lightly in her learned SoCal accent, "you did a huge favor for a friend of mine. And she borrowed something from you at the time. She asked me to return it. Took forever to find you."

Laurie watched Rick process her statement. It had been innocent enough that the woman behind the bar, one Bethany Harcourt-McGregor, should not be able to decipher it.

Rick could. She watched the blood drain out of his face.

Yes. He remembered.

Laurie pulled the bundle out and unwrapped the stainless steel travel mug. Amaleti had considered it her good-luck charm, but had been willing to give it up so that it could be returned to its rightful owner. After the metals shop had fabricated her a perfect replica as a replacement.

Mermaids tended to be stubborn coworkers.

"Well, two things, actually," Laurie said. The cloth bundle itself was a black cloth t-shirt printed with the name of an apparently-now-defunct, small-scale, *punk* band and their logo. She pulled it flat on the top of the bar to study it.

"I've never heard of these guys," she said.

"They broke up about a decade ago," he replied quietly.

She glanced sideways at him. He appeared to be relaxing slowly.

"I'm surprised she didn't keep the shirt," he said after a moment.

"She had it copied," Laurie replied. "Wears it constantly." Well, had the logo printed onto a water-proof dive tunic. Laurie grinned at the memory of the only mermaid on that team wearing anything, and it was a black concert T-shirt from Earth.

The owner, Bethany, finished making her drink and sat it on the bar.

"Rick," she said with a warm smile, "I'll be in back doing paperwork. Yell if you need help."

Suddenly, Laurie was alone with Rick. He seemed even more flustered at the non-verbal interaction with the other woman than he had been with her.

He even blushed to the tips of his ears.

Fascinating. In her mind, she updated her notes on this woman. Obviously, there was more to Bethany Harcourt-McGregor than they had accounted for in their operational notes.

She watched her target set his glass of red wine on the bar and hold a hand out for her to shake. "Hi, I'm Rick."

She grasped it in the human style.

"Laurie Bradley," she said. "Nice to finally meet you, Rick. Heard a lot about you."

He seemed disturbed by her presence. "What can I do for you, Laurie?"

She decided that they were alone enough, if she talked quietly. "We need your help."

Laurie watched the rest of his blood drain out of his face.

"Why me?" he whispered. It sounded almost pained, although she might have been imagining things. Human inter-personal relations were still relatively new to her. She'd been an analyst for the longest time, not a field agent.

She dropped her voice down to the same level of whisper. "Because you are one of the few humans who knows about us, Rick," she said, "and you've proven that you can keep a secret."

"Why not Gustav?" he replied. "He was there too, you know."

Laurie leaned closer, letting the programmed instincts kick in and override her normal behavior. Apparently, this was what it meant to be human.

He even smelled good.

"That's true. He was," she said, "but this is also a serious law enforcement issue and it needs to be resolved without involving human authorities. If we brought him in, his ethics would be tested in ways that we would prefer not to try."

"Jesus," he said, "just how bad could things be that you need me and not a cop?"

She didn't think Rick was actually looking for the raw truth, but she decided that he should know before she involved him any deeper. As it was, she could still walk back out the door and out of his life, having returned his property and thanking him.

That was only ethical.

"One of ours," she said calmly, sternly, forcefully, "has gone rogue, possibly insane, and is committing the most grievous crimes imaginable. I have been tasked with stopping him, but I am normally assigned to Los Angeles and do not know this area very well."

She heard his gasp. His pupils got larger as she watched. From her studies of human physiology, this was the adrenalin rush, the fight-or-flight syndrome that made humans such dangerous combatants.

"Don't you have other people here?" he asked quietly.

And there it was. The file on Rick Pine had indicated a rare combination of extreme intelligence and the ability to draw accurate conclusions on the most flimsy of evidence. Humans called it Intuition.

He was very, very good at it.

"We do, Rick," she replied seriously. "Tarquenic, our rogue agent, has already killed two of them. We pulled everybody else out immediately. They sent me to find him, to stop him, because he does not know me on sight, and because I have been rebuilt to the same capability levels as he has."

"Jesus," came the response.

She decided to press on. It would be highly unethical to ask him to join the danger without full information. "Also, Rick, he has begun to kill humans."

"Humans?" he asked fiercely, biting off all the questions she could see in his eyes.

"Your kind, Rick," she replied. "Apparently, he has decided that he can make humanity better by killing off all the criminals he can locate. There have been a few cases in the local news broadcasts recently. I have to stop him. I would like your help."

She watched two arguments go back and forth on his face. Laurie decided to sit patiently while he processed everything. It was the ethical position.

Long moments passed.

Laurie sipped her mocha, reveling in the warm sweetness.

When she had free time, she really wanted to set up a company on Earth to export beans and all the hardware off-world and introduce the galaxy to coffee culture. It might even convince the galaxy that the humans weren't completely without value.

And it would make her rich. She knew other species would like the stuff almost as much as humans did.

Rick took a deep breath and finished off his wine. "We need to have this conversation somewhere else," he growled at her.

Laurie nodded and stood up. This was already a better outcome than she had assumed, walking in through the door. Humans were extremely unpredictable creatures.

"Bethany," he called out to the other woman, "I'm going to head out with Laurie. Kitchen is clean. Can you lock up?"

Laurie heard the smile in the voice that floated back. The woman Bethany had apparently drawn the obvious, if entirely wrong, conclusion.

"Absolutely, Rick," Bethany called. "You two have fun."

Laurie watched Rick blush again and decided that the relationship between the two humans was even more complicated than it initially appeared. She was apparently being mistaken for a possible girlfriend.

Laurie grinned as she turned and walked to the door to hide her own blush.

Chapter 2

Rick stepped out into the rain and looked both ways. In the pen, that had been just good common sense. Here, he was already twitchy. Might as well run with it.

Let's see. Three other places I can get coffee right now, close enough to swing a dead cat. Besides the bar I just walked out of. Ice cream. Beer. Rain.

I need a cigarette.

Rick fumbled out a pack and pulled a stick and his throwaway lighter. A quick flick and it was burning, sending calmness into his bloodstream. Beside him, the girl gave a disapproving look, but kept her mouth shut. That was a good choice, right this moment.

Okay. Up towards home or down towards town? Ya know what? Water. Trees. What the hell. Four blocks? Half mile? Piece of cake.

Rick crossed 22nd and walked under the big neon sign for the Cult Of The Mermaid. He had to glance over to make sure Laurie was keeping up. She walked completely silently, which was saying something in big, heavy Docs like those. And short legs.

He took another drag and let Market Street stretch out in front of him. Past the smoke shop where he stocked up. Past the licensing place. The yoga den was closed, this late.

Always good to watch the girls in tight, stretchy pants walking around on a nice day.

Down to the light and cross. For a late Sunday night in October, a lot of people still wandering around. Never jaywalk Market. Crazy tourists will run you over in a blink.

Laurie leaned close while he waited for the light to change.

"Do we have a destination, Rick," she asked, "or just a need to exercise?"

He looked over and down as she smiled up at him. *Damn. She was hot. And looked like she wanted a kiss right now. How did I get into this mess? Oh. Right. Mermaid. What the hell is Laurie? I mean, those can't be real, can they?*

Rick grunted. Safer that way.

People walking. Keep up. Cross again. South side of the street. Past the restaurant. Getting into the industrial areas. Fewer people around.

Cute little ghost padding along beside me. Cigarette burned out. Pinch it. Toss it down a gutter. Deep breath. Another mermaid chick. Or whatever the hell she was.

Glance over. Yup. Smoking hot. And a Martian, or something. Slow down. Walk casual. Two people out on a date. No, I am not holding hands with an alien chick. I don't care how nice her tits are.

Shit.

"How the hell are we supposed to find this dude, anyway?" Rick half-whispered. *Yeah. We. Shit. Rick, Dudley Do-Right is going to get you killed one of these days.*

She smiled at him as she kept up with his pace. "There are ways," she said vaguely. "He and I are both machine enough to show up on the right scanners."

Rick stopped dead in his tracks. His eyes wanted to bug out of his head about five sizes bigger, just like they did in the old cartoons. He could feel his mouth made fish motions, opening, closing, opening again.

He turned, but couldn't find any meaningful words. His brain felt like the TV screen when the cable went out. All static and white noise.

Laurie made it worse by just staring up at him calmly, as if she expected rationality to come out of his pie hole.

As if.

Rick took a deep breath. "What are you?" he finally whispered, a lot harsher than he intended.

She smiled wryly. Apparently, that was the question she had been waiting for.

"What do you know about cybernetics, Rick?" she said quietly. For extra fun, she took hold of his hand and tugged him along as she continued west down Market. Now, they really were two cute kids out on a date.

"Cyber-what?" The white noise was back.

"You ever watch Japanese Anime?" She walked slowly, almost dragging him along.

"Huh?" It wasn't getting any better.

"Okay. Did you watch re-runs of the Six Million Dollar Man when you were a kid?"

"The Bionic Man?" Rick's brain finally found something to grasp on to. He held it like a life-preserver in a stormy sea. "You're, like, a robot?"

He watched her hold her right hand out as they walked, palm down, at about the level of her belly button. *It was probably a really cute one, too.*

"Pretty much everything from here down is cybernetic," she said calmly. "I have a few organic parts left. From here up it is mostly organic, with heavily-reinforced bones and a few adjustments to my sensory apparatus."

Yup. White noise. Every one of those words was English. Apparently.

"The outer shell is a cosmetic layer designed to look human, Rick," she smiled and winked at him. "And to distract the male of the species."

"Uhm, yeah. Mission accomplished, lady," Rick replied. Mission really accomplished. "So those aren't real?"

She glanced down at the gap in her jacket. Just enough water had seeped in to plaster her t-shirt to the shape of her overly-done cleavage.

"No," she smiled up at him, "but you'd never be able to tell."

Rick blinked as his brain reset. Or tried to reset.

Great. Alien robot chick from a Japanese cartoon coming on to him. In the rain. It sounded like the opening to one of those semi-fake letters to an advice columnist. The really weird ones.

Rick started to walk again. She held his hand and kept up. *It was going to be one of those nights.*

"So where are we headed?" she asked after another fifty yards passed.

"The Gardens," he replied. Trees. Quiet. Darkness.

He needed some peace before this shit freaked him completely out.

Laurie easily kept the pace as Rick marched. It wouldn't do to tell him that she could out-walk him by orders of magnitude. He was just beginning to relax and warm to her. She needed his assistance here.

This wasn't her town. Hell, it wasn't even her planet. LA she could do. Seattle required a tour guide.

Still, she hadn't realized going in how much fun it would be to flirt with a human. Apparently, her psychological modifications went far deeper than she had originally expected.

In her head, Laurie tried to work out their location. This was the Seattle neighborhood known as Ballard, on the north side of Salmon Bay. The *Hiram M. Chittenden Locks* that connected Lake Washington to the Puget Sound via a series of artificial canals was close by, southwest of her current position, roughly in the direction they were headed.

She resisted the urge to get out her human smart phone and pull up a map. That would involve letting go of Rick's hand at a time he was finally calming. Better to just let him burn the excess energy out of his system. Humans were unpredictable that way. Better to treat them like a particularly intelligent wild animal.

So she kept up with him as they walked several blocks west. Sunday was a quiet day, and this late at night, there was a declining amount of traffic. Having fewer onlookers around would probably help Rick relax.

The season also helped with keeping the crowds down, as a mild October rain fell. In Los Angeles, the predicted overnight low temperature was probably ten degrees warmer than the daily high was going to get up to here in Seattle.

Good thing she had been designed and built for extreme weather.

The road curved here as Market faded into 54th, from the signs. Up ahead, she could see a restaurant/bar next to a long parking lot, with a wall of trees behind a high fence beyond that. If her pacing had been correct, the Locks were just behind those trees.

This really was a pretty neighborhood. LA had nothing like this for greenery, unless you went up to the Observatory, or clear out to Topanga. She needed to visit more often. Green was nice. Weird, but nice.

Soothing.

Rick's destination was apparently close as well, as he turned and walked across the parking lot and a single old railroad right of way. To her left, she could see people apparently camped behind buildings along the rail bed.

Right there, that was why the galaxy hated humans. Their treatment of each other.

Still, that wasn't her mission tonight. She needed to recruit local help to hunt down a killer. She could save humanity tomorrow.

Rick got her attention by cursing.

They stood before a large fence and closed gate, steel posts made to look like old-fashioned wrought iron. *Maybe they were. How quaint.*

Rick continued to curse effusively.

Laurie stepped a little ways to her right, pulling him along absently. She pointed at the sign nearby. "Rick," she said quietly, not trying to override his stream of invective. "The park closes at 9 pm on Sundays. Were you not aware of this?"

He paused and took a deep breath. He scowled fiercely, although it appeared to be centered on himself and not her. He grumbled under his breath.

"Hmm?"

"I said," Rick finally said, "that I never get out on Sundays. Mondays, it's open all day. Crap. Maybe we should just walk over and see my buddy Chet."

She was about to agree to this new destination when she heard a faint beep come from inside her jacket. That was the sensor tuned for cybernetics signatures. It had been set to ignore her, so it should only go off if…

Oh, my. If it was beeping now, it had picked up the only other one of her kind left in Seattle, the man she was supposed to be hunting.

Tarquenic must be close. Close enough that he was hunting her instead.

Chapter 3

He was doing the humans a favor. They were far too short-sighted to realize it, and might not for a very long time. That was acceptable. His cybernetically-enhanced body had been engineered to last for decades before he needed exhaustive maintenance.

Tarquenic glanced into the back-up mirror hung from the center of the glass windshield. It was always a jarring thing, watching the monster that stared back.

Everything but the color of the eyes was wrong. Those were still brown, as the Maker had intended. But the skull was the wrong shape. The eyes were too small.

He had a nose.

And his prominent crest had been removed, planed off with a scalpel, so that hair could be implanted. It even grew, requiring regular visits to a barber. Another exotic perversion in the name of galactic peace.

Tarquenic sighed. He was one of *them* now.

Doctors, cyberneticists, and psychologists had conspired to turn him into a reasonable facsimile of human. That meant living with human thoughts, human ideas, human smells.

They had not explained what it would actually do to him.

Perhaps they were incapable of understanding.

It was crowded, dirty, and maddening on this planet. Humans, for all their vaunted grand dreams, for all of Locke and Jefferson and Gandhi, were clearly insane. Hobbes and Malthus were a better representation.

Worse, they were predators, constantly stalking the weak and doing terrible things to them. Law enforcement had devolved to a tool of the wealthiest to keep entire segments of society under close control.

Politics on this entire planet was a random mechanism to identify who would receive the choicest cuts of offal. In the more advanced nations, democratic transitions apparently served to offer the opposition a chance to feed first for a while, rather than working to upset the apple cart. Less "well-developed" areas just maintained complete iron control until the edifice collapsed, usually along generational lines.

And his people thought that humans could be welcomed into galactic society? Trusted? Clearly, they were even more insane than humans were.

A fist lashed out, slammed hard into the dashboard of the primitive land vehicle, dented it slightly.

Tarquenic took a calming breath.

So much to do. So much that had not been clear until he had come here. Had experienced this world, these animals. Had decided to make this a better place.

The cull had already started.

It had been an accident. No. It had been a sign from the Maker.

One of Seattle poorer neighborhoods. A late night waiting for the rain to start. A badly lit alley. The humans called it a recipe for disaster.

There had been a human with a knife, making threats. Threats became demands. Demands became physical violence. Violence had ignited rage.

Later, standing over the man's body, Tarquenic had marveled at how fragile humans were, or perhaps how much augmentation had been done to his system. It had taken a single blow from a clenched fist to shatter human bones, to end a life.

And blood. A pool of fresh blood spreading out around the cooling corpse.

Then fear. Being caught by the local police authorities. Being found out by his masters. Failure.

Finally, revelation. Not all humans were bad. And he had been chosen as the Maker's instrument to cull them, save them, redeem them.

At last, he understood the apocalyptic overtones of human religion.

Each rabid animal he subtracted from humanity gave them a better chance to evolve into something that could join the galactic community. They were trapped here when they could be helped.

Why had he never seen it before that moment? What else had been hidden from him?

The conspiracy of silence went deep. Neither Garrahn nor Dufelmetriis had been willing to tell him the truth when confronted. Both had tried to suppress him when they discovered that the secret had been opened. Killing them was the only way to keep his own secret knowledge safe.

And now, they had sent another.

This one was much more dangerous. She was another Search-And-Rescue model, like himself. Radically augmented, cybernetically improved, camouflaged to look human.

She was another hunter/killer, another one like him.

Garrahn's files had had a recognition picture of her and some rudimentary information. Useful in emergencies, such as this.

Through the mist, it normally would have been difficult to identify her, especially at a safe distance like this, but Tarquenic had begun to think like the predators he hunted. He could watch and wait.

As humans said, *patience was a virtue.*

Garrahn's files also contained references to three humans in the Seattle urban metroplex that knew about the alien infiltration. One of them owned a small eating establishment nearby.

Tarquenic watched the restaurant from the front seat of his car, legally parked at a public space two blocks away. No human's eyes would be able to see well at this distance. Yet another advantage from his cybernetics.

He watched her approach and enter the restaurant. It was obvious in how she moved that she hadn't been borne as a human.

Tarquenic smiled. The Maker could not have offered him a better opportunity. Ambush her inside a confined space. Slaughter the human that might offer others assistance. There were only eighteen combat models available on this planet. If he killed her now, he might have months before they could bring in another.

He exited his land vehicle and began to walk south on 22nd, a righteous smile on his face.

Old habits were the best kind. Tarquenic reached inside the waterproof outer layer he wore and touched the grip of the beam weapon.

From the other side, he pulled out a small sensor pod camouflaged to look like a late model human smart phone. The sensitivity was lacking at his range, but with some focusing he was able to pick up the signatures of her internal power cells. She would have to know where he was to do the same.

As long as he stayed outside the normal scan range, she wouldn't know he was there.

Hunter/killer began his stalk.

Cross the quiet street. Check both ways to make sure the Public Library had no external security personnel. Verify that the homeless person moving around was in fact harmless and not a decoy.

Tarquenic had considered killing more humans just to make facilities available for the homeless to have someplace to stay.

Perhaps tomorrow.

Now the difficult part. Across the street, anywhere south of the bank, and he might show up on Larek's sensor pod. He would have to move quickly, possibly approach at a dead run so he could get there before she had a chance to react.

Tarquenic took a deep breath and pulled the beam weapon.

A sound stopped him. A bell. The door on the restaurant opened. She emerged, looked around, followed shortly by the human.

Shards, she had already made contact.

Tarquenic froze. Humans reacted to movement.

He counted seventeen other humans within immediate sight, plus an unknown number just around the corners and within the nearby coffee shops and bars. Too many witnesses. If he assassinated her here, there would be a good description of him available to local authorities. And her body would be available to dissect.

Humans must never know they were not unique in the universe.

The knowledge alone would spur them to concentrate on spaceflight and quickly discover the truth. Tarquenic shuddered at stories of Huns, Goths, Conquistadors, and Mongols. The galaxy would not be safe.

That was why the Maker had sent him here. To protect the innocents of all species.

Tarquenic watched Larek and the human cross the street and begin to traverse west on the main street in Ballard. He paced them and walked down to the corner.

There. Passing the industrial area and headed towards the dark industrial areas. Better and better.

Tarquenic holstered the beam weapon and checked his portable sensor pod. Two hundred human meters seemed to be the range to locate Larek. On default, her own pod would pick him up at sixty-three meters.

The hunter/killer smiled and raced back to his land vehicle.

Chapter 4

Rick felt like a moron. Of course the Gardens would close at night. Especially on a Sunday. Had he been thinking, he would have remembered that. This girl was really messing with his calm.

And she just stood there, pleasantly smiling up at him.

Something in her leather jacket beeped. It was a quiet sound. Just one little *meep* in the darkness.

Rick's evening was already in a twitchy place. That just set off all his alarms.

He had turned slightly to his right to look back at Laurie. Behind her, coming down 54th was an older sedan, a 4-door beater that had been blue once upon a time.

It was going too fast.

The driver's window was down.

In this rain.

Absolutely not good.

It swerved into the parking lot, heading right at them.

Suddenly, Rick was back in his Army days, on patrol in a desert sandbox shithole, about to be ambushed. At least then he had been armed. These days, he wasn't allowed anything more dangerous than a boning knife.

A pistol appeared in the window as the wheels screamed.

Really? A drive-by? In Ballard?

The car crossed over the railroad tracks and swerved. Once upon a time, Rick had known a wheelman who could have pulled this stunt. It took skill and timing.

The idiot driving over there was no wheelman.

Rick grabbed Laurie by a sleeve and pulled her with him as he dropped to his knees. Bangers in drive-by mode always shot high. Too much adrenalin, too much momentum, not enough compensation. Not that he'd ever had to do something like that, in his bad old days.

Not at all, officer.

And there went the shot, low and wide and left. Rookie mistake. You have to have a wheelman driving while someone else shoots. Plus cars were prone to slide on the wet pavement and the moron overcorrected both his shot and his driving. Nearly plowed into a parked minivan when he did so.

Nasty beam weapon of some sort. Quiet pulse of light that left afterimages when Rick blinked.

Okay, we've got cover until he backs up or gets out. Or shoots his way through the van, maybe.

Three seconds. Tops.

Move.

Rick was amazed at how quickly the old reflexes were coming back.

Laurie was holding something in her right hand that looked like a pistol. Maybe. Probably a Buck Rogers version. Not time to ask.

"We gotta bug out, lady," he said, moving back to the east along the fence and pulling her along with him.

Pure luck, that first shot had hammered the gate right about the level of the lock. Or his belly-button had he been standing over there.

Wrought iron had a particularly strange smell when it had been flash-heated to failure. Nasty and acrid.

Rick lunged and pushed at the metal, but there was a metal post going down into the concrete. And the whole thing was hot enough to burn. He let go with a curse.

"What is it?" Laurie was right beside him, still moving like a ghost.

"Need to lift there," Rick pointed. "Pull that up and the gate will open. Lots of cover inside, plenty of places to hide."

He glanced back. That guy was just now getting his door open. Either he was slow or Rick was so totally hyped right now that everyone else was in slow motion.

Probably both.

Rick's jaw dropped as Laurie reached into the small gap, still red-hot, and pulled on the sheared-off locking post with a bare hand.

Alien. Robot chick.

She pulled the post clear and pushed the gate open in one motion. Rick could feel the heat from here, but she apparently didn't notice.

"Now what?" she said, taking a step inside the Gardens.

Rick slid by, careful not to touch the metal. "Now we get inside."

He took off at a jog, glancing back to place her as he moved. She kept up.

Okay, in and quick to the right. Left is the sidewalk to the Locks proper. No cover for a hundred yards. Nursery on the right. Trees, bushes, posts, planter boxes. Right it is. Shit, a gun would be nice right about now.

He slipped behind a planter box, ducked down, and caught his breath.

"Rick," Laurie whispered from next to him. "He is stalking us somehow. I am inexperienced in this form of urban combat. Do you have suggestions?"

He glanced over and saw something in her hand that was not holding the gun. It looked like a smartphone, but the dimensions were wrong. It reminded him of an old GPS system, with a blue dot blinking near to the solid purple dot that he assumed was them.

The blinking dot entered the Gardens through the ruined gate.

Laurie confirmed that the weapon was armed and the safety was off. She was left-handed, so she held her portable scanner in her right and watched the icon that was Tarquenic approach.

The device did not have a particularly great range, unless she tuned it. Presumably, Tarquenic had done just that, which had allowed him to find them without being detected in turn.

Internally, she cursed. She was trained in Search & Rescue Operations, not Urban Combat. That was a whole different schooling regime. And she was supposed to be stalking Tarquenic, not the other way around.

How had things gone so bad so quickly?

Rick leaned close to whisper in her ear. He had a nice smell.

"Can that thing shoot through brush?" he asked.

"Through?" she inquired, unclear on the concept. "Ah. No. The pulse liberates on the first solid object it encounters."

"Crap," he replied. "We need a gun."

Laurie glanced down at the scanner. Tarquenic had paused, right at the edge of scan range, and then stepped back.

"Why do we need a gun, Rick?" she asked.

Rick grabbed her arm and tugged her to her feet. "Because it works in brush, rain, and fog. Let's go."

He began to move deeper into the treed area.

"Why do we need to move?" she said as she followed.

"He has one of those, too, right?" Rick pointed at the scanner.

"Yes, most likely," she said as they came to the edge of the arboretum area.

"So he found us with it," Rick said, looking all directions and then down at the scanner, "and is getting ready to rush us. We need to be elsewhere."

"How do you know these things, Rick?"

He didn't answer. Instead, he took off at a sprint across the small open space, over a paved surface, and came to a halt next to an evergreen bramble of some sort. Laurie was several strides back when he started, and right behind him when he came to rest.

"Military training, once upon a time," he said quietly, "plus advanced criminal activity and time in the joint. You learn to read the signs."

"I see," she said. She didn't actually see what he meant, but human vernacular contained that concept. It would be useful to have an expert in human combat close by. Tarquenic shouldn't have any greater tactical and strategic acumen or experience than she did. They needed an edge, if they were going to escape and survive.

She needed Rick, obviously.

"How," she continued after a beat, "do we beat him?"

Rick pointed at the scanner. "Does that work like flashlight, or is it only circular?"

"Like what?" Laurie had trouble following his train of thought.

She considered the portable scanner. Oh. Yes. Directed scan mode.

Tarquenic had spotted her, and had used the directed mode to follow her. Of course.

Rick was using his *Intuition* again. She had an extra weapon in that. She just needed to trust him.

"Here," Laurie handed him the scanner. She pushed the mode button and watched the screen change. "You are now doing Directed Scan instead of General Pulse. Point it like this."

She watched him look up and scan the dark brush that demarcated the edge of the Gardens. If she didn't know better, she would have thought he had sniffed the night air. It had that look about it.

Silently, she watch as Rick held the scanner and aimed it. He made a quick pass right to left, and then a slower pass back.

Yes. Intuition. He understood that sensitivity was proportional to motion.

There. Tarquenic. Close to fence, moving laterally. Possibly inside, possibly outside. Difficult to determine.

How do you sneak up on someone who can see you coming?

Tarquenic had relied on speed and surprise. It would have worked had Rick not been able to maneuver. She would be dead now, but for him.

Interesting. Another alien woman who owed Rick Pine her life.

She felt Rick's hand on her shoulder, wanting to turn her to face deeper into the park. She resisted, stronger than he was.

"What are you doing?" she asked.

He pointed at another patch of green, shadowed in the darkness.

"Run there next," he said as he raced off.

Laurie kept up easily, a little confused by the situation, but willing to trust the human. And learning quickly.

The next batch of cover was longer. They moved through it noisily, but quickly.

Rick stopped at the far edge and looked up and down the long concrete walkway. Ahead, Laurie could see the massive steel and concrete construction that was the Locks, spanning Salmon Bay and providing an artificial output for Lake Washington. The spillway dam ran all the way across the water.

Ah, an escape path, and one that limited Tarquenic's options to pursue them.

She started to take a step, but Rick's hand on her shoulder held her back.

Laurie turned to see what he was trying to communicate. She found him facing back the way they had come.

The mist was heavier now. It might actually begin to degrade the range capabilities of the beam weapon if it got worse.

She turned to find Rick studying her face closely. She discovered that she had apparently inherited the ability to blush like a human.

"I need you to trust me," he said, calmly.

Laurie felt her eyebrows rise involuntarily. Again, another programmed response related to humanity. It was interesting to actually *be* one, now. Watching from the inside, as it were.

So much of their communication was apparently non-verbal. She wasn't sure how many analysts had understood that. Obviously, she had missed a great deal up until now.

Rick pointed at the beam weapon. "I want to bait a trap," he said.

"A trap?" she replied, lost.

"Yes," he nodded. "That guy's tracking you with one of these." He held up the portable scanner. "Can he see me?"

"No," Laurie said. Suddenly, enlightenment dawned. Tarquenic would not be able to locate Rick if she moved away from him. They could separate, and Rick could escape. It was a good plan.

She nodded.

"Good," Rick said. "I need the pistol."

What? Why? A human with access to a beam weapon? That violated every tenet of the Observation Mission. She would be Censured when the authorities found out. Demoted. Cast out. Fired.

"You run," he continued, watching the emotions play out on her face. Again, human physical communication. "He chases you. I'm invisible. I shoot him when he goes by."

Oh. The human solution. Violence. Destruction.

Still, Tarquenic had embraced violence as a medium of communication. And I have been sent to stop him. At this point, was there any other method available to achieve my goals except by resorting to absolute barbarity?

She had to fight her own hand. It nearly refused to hold the weapon out. So many policy violations. *What was one more? She was going to be fired anyway, even if she somehow managed to survive this.*

Rick wrapped his warm hand around hers and took the pistol. He appeared to instinctively understand how it worked, as he held his index finger well away from the firing stud and placed his thumb next to the safety. *Were the tools of violence instinctive? Were humans programmed to violence? So much she didn't know.*

"Does it have any recoil" he asked.

Why would it have recoil? Ah. Ignited-gunpowder weapons generated pressure to launch a projectile. Recoil came when the slug exited the barrel and the pressurized exhaust gases had to be vented. Humans lacked beam weapons. Or had.

"No," she said after a beat. "Point the barrel and pull the trigger. It will fire a single pulse and cycle in approximately three-quarters of a second."

"Good," he replied, pointing across the walkway to more bushes and a building. "You run there, count to five, and then sprint across the spillway. Do not stop. Do not look back. When you cross, climb the hill through

Commodore Park. If I'm not with you at that point, continue to the top of the hill and look for the Fort Lawton Military Cemetery. I'll find you there."

She felt his hand on her hip, trying to move her.

She considered a response. She had seen it in one of her favorite human movies.

She couldn't resist.

Laurie leaned forward and kissed a very surprised Rick on the mouth. "For luck."

And then she ran.

Rick sat there stunned.

Damn it. Why did she have to go do that? What the hell was wrong with her? And what the hell was wrong with him?

Okay, deep breath.

Watch her run. Nice bottom. Good form.

Sit perfectly still. Another little dark bump in the mist.

Rick remembered playing these sorts of games in the neighborhood when he was a kid. Only then, it had been squirt guns.

And rules. No rules here.

Rick scanned with the weird little GPS-thingee until he found a radar echo.

There. Movement. Hi, asshole.

Rick watched a man's shadow emerge from deeper in the park. Somewhere over there was a house, sitting perfectly in the middle of the Gardens, but privately owned. Rick had no idea who lived there, or how it came to be. Probably the original guy in charge of the locks when they were built, so long ago.

This didn't look like a retiree with money. He moved like a predator. Low, quiet, fast. He appeared human, but Rick knew better than to assume anything at this point.

The guy carried a gun and a scanner just like Laurie's as he moved. Rick watched his head bob down as he watched the screen, then up to watch his step. Down. Up.

Apparently, never played midnight tag when he was a kid.

Rick smiled as the shadow slipped by him across the clear space. Four quick steps and the alien dude was across the pavement into some brush next to the stairs down to the water.

Out of the corner of his eye, Rick caught movement as Laurie made her break. He turned to make sure she had gotten across the first lock and then turned back.

The guy was gone.

Shit.

Rick looked down at his scanner device.

There.

Crap. The restrooms are in the way.

Okay, across and run into him, or lateral and catch him coming out?

Rick stepped onto the pavement and jogged sideways towards the main building in the middle of the quad, trying to watch Laurie, and his footing, and the brush over there.

The guns were amazingly quiet.

Rick heard the faintest hum and hiss, but that might have been the rain. Down on the spillway, however, a chunk of iron railing vaporized with a shattering crack.

Rick saw Laurie stagger as she ran, then start to zig and zag

Rick stopped, right in the middle of the open and frantically looked for the shooter.

Don't look down. Eyes on the target. Shoot at movement. Pursue. Just like in the desert.

Rick saw something. This late at night, in the rain, trespassing in a closed park, he was willing to gamble that there weren't going to be any innocent bystanders around.

He fired.

The weapon had no more recoil than a laser pointer. It felt like a gun, so he had held it like one.

The shot went into the ground at the guy's feet as the alien dude stepped forward for his second shot, instead of catching him low in the torso like it was supposed to.

Zero kick. One hell of a downrange. I need one of these.

An area of sod and concrete a few feet across simply exploded, superheated by the impact of the weapon.

Rick was blinded for a second by the strobe of light.

He had just enough night vision left to see the guy get knocked sideways by the shockwave, out of sight.

Not good. Wounded bad guy down in the bush. Do not go in there after him.

Rick had had that lesson pounded into him repeatedly by his sergeant. He shifted further to his left, got a building between them in case the guy was playing possum.

Rick looked down at the scanner. Somehow, he had managed to reset the controls. Now it just showed him in the middle of a big circular pulse instead of the flashlight mode he had. The little purple dot that was the bad guy was moving towards the edge of the screen in a hurry.

The writing looked like some weird mix of Chinese and Sanskrit. Rick had no way to get it back to what it had been without the girl. Hell, smartphones were almost beyond him right now, after so long in prison, but he was getting better.

Paranoia got the better of him. Rick zipped across the concrete, back toward the bushes by the long entryway. From there, he had a great view down the long paved driveway.

Only, the rain had decided to get worse.

It had stepped up from an ugly mist to a full squall in the last five seconds. Rick's shell was dry enough for now, but he couldn't see much in the dark.

Movement.

Rick pointed and shot, hoping he hadn't just killed someone's dog. *Self-defense, pal. Deal with it.*

Nothing. Not even pretty special effects. Crap tons of steam and sizzle, like the raygun just shorted on all the rain. She had said it liberated on the first thing it touched instead of penetrating. Apparently, rain counted.

Okay, gotta get closer.

A little voice in his head called him all sorts of bad names as he stepped from cover and raced back over to the bushes he had first hidden in. He ignored it, mostly. They sounded like his old sergeant, anyway.

A sudden snap of noise coming at him like a runaway semi.

Heat.

Steam like a Swedish sauna everywhere.

Okay, that's what it feels like when bad guys shoots at you with the Buck Rogers gun. Totally different from the desert.

Rick slid into the bushes with his head on a swivel. He looked down, but the scanner was blank.

Okay, the other guy couldn't sneak up on him if he paid attention.

And they were too far apart to shoot each other unless the rain stopped.

A gun would be really nice right about now.

Rick considered getting closer. He had trained as a boxer and learned some martial arts in the pen. It had been both self-preservation and something to do, before he had taken a class on cooking and been bitten by the bug to be a chef.

Then he remembered Laurie sticking her hand through the bars to open a gate that was still red-hot. And the guy over there was built just as tough.

Yeah, getting in close to this guy was a good way to get my ass kicked.

Rick checked the scanner. Blank. He couldn't see Laurie on the bridge either. Hopefully she had gotten away. He could find her easy enough later.

Oh, what the hell.

Rick braced his feet on the slippery grass. He could smell the wet everywhere, once he stopped to think about it.

He ran, hard, pivoted, ran again, paused, zagged.

Bad guy fired a shot that went well wide and probably wouldn't have killed him anyway, given the amount of steam it generated.

Nasty warm, though. Almost smelled like wet dog in here. Rick figured that was his own scent, cranked up after so long behaving.

It kinda felt good to be in action again. He'd have to control that feeling. That addictive seduction of violence. Too easy to fall into the bad ways and go back to the joint.

Never.

Rick found cover by the house. It had a low fence all the way around, with enough brush to keep everything hidden both ways.

He looked down at the GPS-thingee and had a signal, right at the edge.

Gotcha, asshole.

Slide along the near side or loop around back? What was that guy looking for from him?

Rick gasped hard as he thought, a combination of adrenalin overdrive, too many cigarettes, and not enough exercise.

Have to work on that. Chef-ing is hard work, always on your feet, but mostly standing still over a hot stove. Not a lot of sprinting.

Still, he had a bead on the alien. There.

Let's go wide. Always try to drive him out onto the locks where there was no cover.

Rick moved.

The brush was wet with a lot of rain by now. It was beginning to mush the ground as well. He felt each step sink halfway deep in the mud. He squelched noisily, but there was nothing to do but keep his eyes on the scanner and make sure he didn't wander from cover into a bolt.

Stop. Breathe. Get your heart under control.

Rick looked at the scanner again. Bad guy moving along the building with the bathrooms, but on the other side.

Rick scampered across the pavement, slipped as he reached grass, and gracefully face-planted into a bush. Reflex brought a hand up to protect his face from branches.

After he blinked the water and leaves out of his eyes, Rick realized that he had dropped the GPS-thingee somewhere in the bush.

A sound brought his head around. Bad guy had just stepped around the building on the other side and was looking right at him. Or right at the bushes.

Rick prayed as he snapped off a shot.

Again, it was low.

The damned thing felt like a 9mm semi-auto, and shot like a garage door opener.

The bolt hit the edge of the building at about knee height, low and right.

There was a tremendous flash of light and shattering of concrete. Rick threw himself flat in the mud, expecting a return shot.

After a moment, nothing happened.

Rick rolled onto his side and aimed downrange, looking for a target.

The rain was thinning. Visibility was up over fifty yards now and gaining every heartbeat.

Rick finally saw the guy, running away. From here, he looked like he was moving at something like forty miles an hour. Rick thought about taking a shot anyway, but had no idea how far away he could hit something with the pistol. Plus, he would be firing blind into the darkness, and would hit someone or something in Ballard if he missed.

Okay. Call it a draw. Found the bad guy, scared him off.

In the distance, the lovely, precious sound of wailing sirens coming closer.

Let's see: breaking and entering, destruction of public and private property, trespassing. And, best of all, felon in possession of a firearm.

No, thank you.

Rick stood up and tried to squelch some of the water and mud off his front, not that it was doing any good.

He gave up and rooted around in the bush until he found Laurie's bug-finder. At least he could locate her easier when he got to the cemetery.

Rick did the math quickly and figured he had time for a cigarette before he needed to bug out.

He patted a pocket and pulled out the crushed pack of soggy cigarettes, and a broken plastic lighter. No point in leaving evidence with finger-prints where they might be found.

He stuffed everything back in his pocket with a particularly colorful stream of quietly-snarled invective. It just kept getting worse.

First rain. Then a training exercise in the rain. At night. A gunfight with an alien dude. Now he was out of cigarettes.

Rick set off to get his butt across the spillway so he could find Laurie. Then he was going to have to find a convenience store and buy some more cigarettes.

It had taken a while. He was finally angry.

Chapter 5

Rick's plan had worked.

Laurie raced through the developing rain at a good clip. There had been only the one shot, and then nothing as she made her escape across the waterway.

The concrete was wet, but her boots were well suited to it. She mentally added her Docs to the list of things she would export from this planet, given the option.

She wondered how the company would have managed to adapt their standard design for her original foot, all toes and barely any heel. Maybe she should just license the trademark instead and hire someone back home to manufacture them. Twenty-ring laces were such an improvement over anything she had had as a youngster.

On the spillway, she passed the fish ladder, turned right, and found herself in a small water-side park. She moved across the slippery grass and back down the slope to a patch of trees near the water's edge. That would protect her from being seen, not that she could see much.

Laurie considered her original instructions, which she had followed to the letter. Two hard days overland drive from Los Angeles to Seattle on her motorcycle, stopping only for food, fuel, and sleeping in Santa Rosa. No contact with any of the local team, since there was no way to tell how much of the network had been compromised. No contact with her superiors until she had established herself in Seattle and was prepared to begin the hunt.

This was probably not what they had meant, but she was loathe to call for help now. It would smack of rank amateurism if she got in over her head so quickly, even if she had.

Something had gone wrong. Where?

What was more interesting, and more concerning, was the fear that things up at the Observation Station on Earth's Moon were not right. Did Tarquenic have supporters in *The Collective* who were in a position to secretly help him? Had she been supposed to fail from the outset?

There were factions that felt humans were too dangerous to even survive as a species, let alone be welcomed into galactic society.

Had she been set up?

Laurie had no answers, and no way to get them. And right now, she needed to survive long enough to be able to ask those questions to the right people. The magnitude of the issue had not even penetrated her conscience until five minutes ago.

Over in the Gardens, a small war continued unabated. Several times, she heard the whip-crack of the beam weapon pistol as the bolts liberated all their energy on a target. Each time was presaged by a flash of bright light.

Laurie's modified eyes were good enough to catch an after-image each time, so she could see Rick and Tarquenic stalking each other, if only briefly. Neither man seemed to be winning, but she was confident that she would have been killed already if she had had to engage Tarquenic alone.

She considered waiting here to see if there was an outcome, but Rick's instructions had been specific, and she wasn't sure if he would follow her across the dam, or find another way.

She pulled out her locally-issued smart phone and activated the map application. The cemetery Rick had referred to was not far away, but appeared to be at the top of the hill behind her, with no direct roads to get there, and her bike was where she had left it by the bistro. Still, there were parkways, greenbelts, that connected where she was to that area. Laurie quickly memorized the path, put her phone away, and set out to hike.

Across the way, she could hear the wail of sirens as the police responded to strange noises and happenings in the Gardens. From outside the park, it had probably sounded like lightning, or really big cats fighting. One had to know what the beam weapons sounded like to appreciate the sound.

Hopefully, Rick had survived. This would be a difficult chase if she had to go after Tarquenic without him.

Rick squelched as he walked. There was no other way to describe it. His sneakers were amazingly comfy working for hours in a kitchen, but they weren't waterproof. And his socks were just yucky right now.

Still, he had gotten away from a lunatic with a drive-by fetish and survived a grown-up game of tag with laser pistols. In the desert, it had always been dry and gritty when he got back from a patrol. That would be nice right about now. He needed a shower. Dry clothes would be a bonus, too.

And a pony, while he was wishing.

First, he had to get scarce. Fortunately, the rain and the hour had driven most people indoors. He knew a back way up the hill, up a dead-end street to a pedestrian bridge that would drop him off above the tracks. He just needed to not look like a drowned rat getting through these little yuppie neighborhoods. Especially with a gun in his pocket.

She felt like she should be doing something right now, but Rick's instructions had been precise. Get here, wait for a certain period of time for him to catch up. They would plan from there, depending on what had happened below.

That was the most important thing Laurie could do, be here for him to find when he arrived. He would be able to locate her, even if she was operating in the dark. Metaphorically, not physically. Her eyes were still better than anything a human had.

Laurie took a calming breath and sat perfectly still at the edge of the clearing, waiting and watching the quiet white stones and doing the meditations her first human martial arts teacher had taught her.

All that time spent in survival school had paid off, even if she had never expected to do a wilderness exercise in the middle of a major human city. She had a tree at her back, dark jacket zipped up tight, dark jeans, and had pulled a scarf from a pocket to wrap around her head.

She was prepared, even if she was totally lost and confused right now.

She was Search and Rescue. Her superiors called her in when a field sociologist got into trouble in the deserts or the Inland Empire. Who could she contact, if she got in trouble with the local authorities?

Were there even lawyers she could call for this particular situation?

She snorted. Five minutes after she got arrested, they would call in secret government types and she would disappear from the records.

Shards, she had managed to stumble into an absolute worst-case scenario.

Laurie had seen the contingency planning that would make her extraction from human custody look like a major terrorist incident, with or without her body. Right now, she regretted not giving Rick her phone number in all the excitement.

Still, at the time, that probably would have been too forward, too nervy. She had felt his heart start pounding with adrenalin just when she held his hand. Flirting had been useful and fun, but she needed a partner, not a… whatever it was.

Would humans consider that bestiality? Would her kind?

Best not to go there.

Wait for Rick. Get someplace safe where they could plan. Figure out the next step. The local network had obviously been completely compromised, if Tarquenic knew enough about Rick to stake out his restaurant. There was nobody else available as backup.

And, Shards, if she called her superiors for help now, they might just send her back to the desk job as a total failure. Somewhere out there, a human was running around with a portable scanner and a beam weapon.

It was bad enough that one of her kind had gone rogue, gone native. That happened occasionally. They were normally harmless when they did so.

It seemed to sometimes be a response to more primitive societies. Some agents just went native. They usually ended up worshipped as gods or wizards. In response, you sent in a dragon, created a new destruction/creation myth, and went about your business, one chastened agent forcibly deported off-world until they could be given a good talking too.

Here, Tarquenic was killing people, both human and alien. There was a serious gap in contingency planning to throw her in with minimal intelligence and just hope she prevailed.

She wondered again. Was this was all a just set-up for her fail and make humans seem too dangerous to live? Political games someone was playing upstairs?

Laurie wondered if someone up there had prepared a large rock as an emergency bolide strike to destroy the planet and she was just a stalking goat. Nothing like an Act of God to make a point, especially for the people who hated and feared humans to begin with. Wipe the slate clean and start over with a perfectly inhabitable planet?

They wouldn't do that, would they?

A sound distracted that train of thought. It sounded like a whistle, or a bird call.

From her right.

Total darkness. At least the rain had passed. Was that movement?

"Laurie?" Rick's voice floated quietly out of the darkness. "Is that you?"

Laurie let go a breath she hadn't realized she was holding and stood up. She pulled the scarf from her face and took a step to one side, away from the bole of the tree.

She suddenly remembered that Rick had the scanner, so he knew she was there, but hadn't been sure if Tarquenic had snuck up here ahead of him. Was there a gun pointed at her right now? What would he do?

She took a deep breath and moved further into the clearing. "Rick? Here," she said, waiting for a shot.

Rick appeared across from her, muddy and rather the worse for wear. She could see the beam weapon held loosely in his right hand, down along his hip. Discrete, but prepared. And he didn't shoot her, so hopefully he didn't hold her responsible for the way the evening had turned out.

"He got away," he said as he staggered tiredly towards her.

"*We* got away," she replied, closing the gap. "Now we need to get to a secure facility where you can get cleaned up before you are subject to illness."

He stopped, took a breath, and studied her.

"I need to rest before I go climb a barbed-wire fence again." He held out the pistol for her to take, followed by the scanner.

He looked like hell.

"Here," she took his hand after she pocketed her equipment, "let me show you this amazingly comfortable tree I found."

She sat him down and leaned him back while she kneeled close by. Up close, he was steaming from the exertion of climbing the hill while soaked.

Laurie set the scanner down between them, on and listening, just in case. She pulled her human smart phone from another pocket. They needed someplace to stay. It had to be close enough to walk. She smiled to herself and let human technology do the work for her.

There. A chain hotel with vacancies advertised. The rates were even reasonable, although it wasn't her money. And they had laundry facilities and complimentary breakfast. Good.

Distance. Hmm. A little over four miles walk, to nearly downtown and the waterfront. Still, it was the closest place where they could get his clothes cleaned without a lot of questions. And the walking would keep him warm.

Now they needed to move, to be active, to start hunting.

Laurie clicked the button to make a reservation, memorized the route, and looked up at Rick.

He was asleep. That surprised her. She still thought of humans as semi-feral cats, mostly civilized, but still a little crazy and unpredictable at the best of times. *Twitchy.*

He had trusted her enough to return the weapon, and now slept within arm's reach of her, untroubled.

He must be more tired than she had imagined.

From what she understood, a chef/cook job involved being on your feet moving back and forth in a hot kitchen for a number of hours. Such had been his day before she entered his bistro.

Add a small war atop that, and a hike to the top of a hill while soaking wet. Laurie imagined her own cybernetic legs would be complaining at that point.

She let him rest and checked her various email accounts for updates.

Coming here, she had been instructed to maintain what the humans called radio silence, on the assumption that Tarquenic might be able to intercept messages. And there was no backup available if something went wrong.

She smiled down at Rick, still troubled.

How had it gone so wrong? Had she been set up by someone who didn't share her upbeat opinion of human possibility?

So many questions. No answers. And nowhere to get help. Or rather, only this one human to help. She would need to protect him like her life depended on it.

It did.

Chapter 6

The parking lot was a sea of police cars and news station vans. Detective Hall got out of the sedan and looked at the scene with disgust. Her whole life seemed to be getting out of cars at crime scenes. She looked forward to retiring one of these days, where she could get out of a car and shop instead.

That wasn't today.

She looked over at her partner. "Why are we down here in Ballard, Murray? It's late. It's Sunday. And there's no corpse."

Detective Murray had a pensive look about him, the kind he got when he was up to no good. She knew it well.

He fixed her with a beady, piercing eye and let the moment hang.

"'Cause I asked Sgt. Robinson to be on the lookout for weird shit and to call me," he finally explained.

"Define weird, you hillbilly," Hall replied with a biting smile. They had seen and done some very weird shit in their years together. Seattle was a strange place.

Instead of a reply, Murray walked over to the tape and flashed his badge to gain access. Hall followed in his wake, happy to give him his head. Their first stop was the Lock's front gate.

Murray squatted down and got his nose right up against the black iron, like he was part bloodhound. Then again, maybe he was.

She watched him tap the metal with his pen in a few different places, and then point as he looked back and up at her.

"Weird," he said triumphantly.

Hall leaned over his shoulder to see what had this curmudgeon so excited.

The gate was a big thing, cast out of wrought iron bars that had been updated with a modern lock and plate to keep the amateurs out. The plate and lock were badly damaged, almost melted in place.

"So someone blow-torched their way in," she said finally. "Why is that weird?"

"Because someone that knew how to use an oxy-cet torch wouldn't cut here," he pointed at all the damage, off-center on the lock itself, before shifting his pen. "I'd cut here and here. Sixty seconds and I'm in. This would have taken me twenty minutes to get through."

A burly man interrupted before Murray could continue. "It gets worse inside, Murray."

Detective Hall cocked an eyebrow at him. "Really, Lt. Pedrotti,? she purred. "Bad enough to excite Murray?"

Pedrotti grinned at her. Murray had been his partner before being hers. They shared an inside joke.

"Yepper," Pedrotti replied. "Whatever did that did the same thing a couple of places inside. Ain't no torch."

Murray stood, shook his old partner's hand. "Heya, Harvey," he growled with a smile. "You know I love a good mystery."

"Yeah, kid," Lt. Pedrotti replied as he poked Murray in the chest. "No smoking on my crime scene."

Murray grunted but held his own counsel.

Hall could see the wheels turn in his head.

Finally, he cocked his head at the Lieutenant. "About an hour ago?" he asked. "Witnesses?"

Pedrotti shook his head. "None," he said. "Right about the time a squall line come through."

"But dry since then, right?" Murray asked with a tight smile.

Pedrotti nodded.

Detective Hall knew better than to inquire. She just trailed Murray back across the parking lot. Pedrotti did the same. He knew, too.

They both watched Murray approach the nearest vehicle, a green minivan, and put his hand flat on the hood for a moment with his face all screwed up in concentration.

The second vehicle was a faded blue four-door from the age of American cars the size of small countries. Murray put his hand on the hood and held it there.

"This one's still warm," he looked at them expectantly.

Pedrotti shrugged. "You want in?" he said, taking in Hall with his look.

She shrugged back at him. "Not sure I have a choice at this point," she said quietly. "Farm-boy's got a bone in his mouth now. Easier to let him chew it than to try and take it away from him."

"I feel ya, Eleanora," Pedrotti smiled and pointed. "Bunch of homeless back up the tracks. Maybe they saw something."

Murray had already written the plates down. Right now, he had stuck his head in the open window someone had forgotten to close, in spite of the rain. She heard him mutter to himself as he worked.

So much for getting to bed at a reasonable hour.

At least he was happy. That would make him easier to deal with for a while, even if the shit was likely to get weirder.

Chapter 7

Bethany finished doing the books for the day and enjoyed herself a few sips of Syrah. It had been a very good day, and a very good week. If they kept this up, it was going to be a very good year. She might even convince Rick to actually buy a car instead of walking everywhere or taking the bus.

Not that you needed a car in Ballard. But she lived in Wallingford. And Rick was going to need to move up in the world when this place was a success, at least until they were so successful he could go be a Bohemian somewhere, like Ravenna or Magnolia.

Bethany took a last walk around the bistro, making sure everything was put away, off, or closed. Gwen would the first one in on Tuesday to prep everything for dinner, and she didn't appreciate being left a mess.

Outside, the rain had passed. Just another hard Seattle squall. Nothing, then a little mist, then five minutes of utter monsoon, and then nothing. It left the streets clean and drove people indoors. Here, Ballard was in the process of rolling up the sidewalks and going to bed. Another Sunday night in paradise.

Bethany pulled her long, black, leather topcoat from the hook. One did not wear it so much as step into it. But it was very warm, very dry. And it made her look good, which was also important. She slid a few papers into her briefcase, grabbed her keys, and flipped off the lights.

Once the front door was locked up tight, she slid the keys into her pocket and glanced carefully around. In her right hand, hidden in the pocket, she kept a nifty little stun gun her daughter had bought her when Ingrid had learned she was opening a bistro with a former felon.

As if she hadn't had Rick Pine wrapped around her little finger five minutes after they met. Ingrid obviously still needed to learn a few things about handling men. Bethany smiled a wicked little smile to herself as she started up 22nd.

She had long since made a deal with a private parking lot a block away. Her black Mercedes SL had a nice safe spot off the street, between the taco place and the bank, with a lot of foot traffic in the neighborhood and good people around.

Often, Rick had walked her to the car anyway as a bodyguard, but it wasn't far, and he had himself a date tonight. He needed it. She was going to have tease him mercilessly on Tuesday. She smiled even broader. This place was good for what had ailed her since Charles had died.

The street was dark and quiet. Not many homeless here. They tended to congregate down by the water. Still, the alley behind the shoe repair place had a hedge and really poor lighting. So she carried her stun gun in her hand as she walked. A good zap, a scream, maybe a few kicks with her stiletto heels and she'd be away. Plus, Market was a block away and there were always people around.

Bethany squared her shoulders and started north. Her heels clicked on the pavement, but wearing flats in public was just unacceptable. She just had to be careful and stay well away from the building until she was passed. Easy enough.

A glance as she walked. Dark, but not the ominous darkness that might be hiding someone. Just dumpsters and back doors, slick with fresh rain.

A sound.

Footsteps approaching.

But far too fast for someone running.

And coming from her left, across the street.

Bethany had time to look the other direction before something, someone, barreled into her.

Arms around her, impossibly strong, lifting her off the ground bodily.

She had time to twist the little stun gun and push it against the arm holding her.

Sparks and crackles.

No response.

Suddenly, she was cast bodily against a brick wall, driving the breath from her lungs before she could scream.

A man loomed over her, almost as big as her football-playing little brother.

A hand reached for her.

Again with the stun gun. Grind it into him. Hold the trigger.

Nothing.

No, something.

The man wrenched the weapon from her hand, inspected it while she gasped for air.

She finally caught her breath to cry for help.

He lunged at her.

A fist.

Darkness.

Chapter 8

Detective Hall scowled out the windshield as they drove around. They were down in the seedy parts of SODO above Georgetown and the airport. She could see some rich guy's private jet taking off from Boeing Field and banking out over her head.

"Murray," she inquired again, "you sure we're in the right place?" It wasn't the sort of place somebody lived. There were a few really old houses around, but the blocks around here were all small warehouses and light industry. Where you'd go to find a vacuum repair store, or an Indonesian grocery, or, more likely, a chop shop or a drug warehouse.

It wasn't a neighborhood regular people lived, unless they had lived here for fifty years already and were going to die in the house and then let their grandkids sell it to some developer.

She felt his shrug without actually seeing it. They'd been partners long enough.

"Told you, El," he growled quietly. "Looking for weird shit. Whatever the hell happened at the Locks, plus a car that looks suspicious, with an owner who lists that place as his residence." He pointed at an old red-brick place, down two blocks, that had most recently been a repair garage of some sort, a few years ago.

Now it had that seedy run-down look of old abandoned light industrial, but none of the trash and graffiti she would have expected if nobody was actually around. The wood parts had been painted maroon once, maybe that stain that was so popular in the seventies, but it had faded. There were obvious spots where some local punk had tagged it, but they had been covered over pretty well, and nothing looked recent.

Whoever was here, the locals left them alone. That in itself made her wonder. Even bored punks would eventually get around to a place like this, unless they had a reason not to.

Eleanora had never worked this neighborhood, but it reminded her of some of the quieter, older places around Rainier Beach.

Murray revved the engine and they accelerated down the block and turned to the right, away from the building he had pointed at.

"You're really going to sneak up on them tonight?" she cocked an eye at him, happy she had taken to wearing black leather hiking boots around him instead of sensible shoes, especially when Detective Murray had one of his *moments*.

Her husband had teased her mercilessly about the footwear at first, until he came to realize how much better her mood was when she got home from those late night haunts with Murray. And those two men were peas in a pod when they got together, although she was glad Dave worked at the Lazy B and not someplace with as weird of hours as she had to keep.

He, at least, got to bowl regularly with his league. She'd had to give that up years ago.

But being a detective was way more fun anyway.

Murray smiled at her. "Normal people live normal lives and cast normal shadows," he said. It was an old phrase. It had driven more than one of his partners nuts, over the years. But he was also very, very right.

"I know," she replied. "And I'm with you. This ain't normal. Not enough to make him stand out most of the time, but it looks hinky when the lights come on."

"Told you so," he said and then clammed up.

She let him win this round and watched the neighborhood as Murray drove once around the larger radius, and then found a spot, a few blocks over to park.

"Whatcha think, El?" he said finally.

"I want vests on," she replied absently. "Area like this they might shoot first. Big yellow letters that say *Police* will make most of them play nice. And the ones who won't weren't going to anyway."

She opened her door and stepped out as she heard him pop the trunk open.

It was quiet. She had expected to hear dogs barking. But it was amazingly silent. You could live here for a long time and not worry about things.

She snorted to herself. *Yeah, good luck with that.*

At the back of the car, she pulled out her Police vest and put in over her rain shell. Things looked like they were drying out, but the jacket was dark and warm, especially over her body armor and trauma plate. She tapped it once, right between her breasts, for luck, like she did every time she expected to draw her pistol.

Murray cocked his head at her and pulled out his own vest. Everyone had their rituals that brought them home at night. She watched him draw his sidearm, open the slide just enough to confirm that there was a round in the chamber, and slip it back into his shoulder holster.

"Ready?" he said quietly.

"Your idea, Murray," she replied. "You first."

He nodded, scanned his entire neighborhood once by pivoting in place, and then set out for a nearby alley that cut onto the block they wanted.

She trailed in his wake carefully. It was just too quiet around here.

Chapter 9

Laurie stepped around the corner and looked at Rick, shivering in the shadows. The long walk had warmed him up some, and dried him out, but not enough, and standing there still damp was risking illness. She smiled and showed him the white plastic key.

"It is imperative," she said, taking his hand and pulling him towards the stairwell, "that you get warm and dry before you are beset with illness."

He gave her a strange look, which she chalked up to the language. She was falling back into the vernacular of analysis, rather than the patois of the streets she had learned. The situation was undermining her normal functionality in discombobulating ways.

"Warm and dry, Rick," she continued as they mounted the stairs.

The room was a small slice of elegant heaven.

The Collective had established her cover identity well enough that she could function in a modern, electronic society as a consultant and be well-paid in human currencies, just for this sort of situation. Laurie traveled frequently and explored various settings in her role as a Search-And-Rescue field agent, for those times when researchers exploring their ethnographies got into trouble.

That she was the one in trouble here, and there was nobody she could call, weighed on her, but she was a grown-up. She had physical capabilities far beyond what the humans could match, more than enough to go toe to toe with Tarquenic if push came to shove.

And Rick had already proven to be a far greater resource than she hoped. They could do this.

She closed the door and poked him in the chest. "I need all your clothes, Rick," she announced. "There are laundry machines in the basement, so I can get it all clean and dry. You go take a long, hot shower while I throw your things in to wash."

He looked at her for a second with an unreadable face, and then pulled off his jacket.

Laurie tried to watch him clinically as the shirt came off. She was worried about his health, after all. But the smell of him was warm and rich.

Certain areas of her brain reacted in ways she had not encountered before in her human form. The limbs were in all wrong proportions, all leg, and much broader chest and shoulders. And body hair still shocked her, especially as much as he had on his chest and the line that trailed down his stomach.

He was extremely lean and spare. Apparently his stint in prison had left him with the time to work out regularly in his cell and maintain much better muscle tone than the average human male.

Much better.

Laurie collected his pants and socks and stuffed them into a laundry bag along with the rest. "Back in a few minutes," she said as she made her way to the door.

Outside, in the hallway, she leaned back against the wall for a second and took a deep breath. The new human parts of her brain wanted to stick her nose into the bag and take a deep smell of Rick's musk. The older, alien, parts were aghast. She listened to them argue the back of her mind for a few moments before she went ahead and did it anyway.

The result was a pure jolt of adrenalin to the base of her brain stem.

Had they programmed her too well?

Laurie shook her head and stepped away from the wall.

These were just protective sub-routines kicking in, after all. He was your partner.

Right?

Rick stared at the closed door and blinked.

Seriously? Alien cyborg assassin chick had been looking at him like a squirrel who had found a pretty awesome tree she wanted to climb. Part of his brain started listening again, for the porn music to start grinding up.

It had been a very, very long time since he had been with anyone. But man, she wasn't even human, as much as she looked like one.

Rick let go a long breath and walked into the bathroom. He cranked the handle over as hot as it would go and stepped back to wait.

In prison, you had one choice on water temperature. Kinda luke warm that was enough to get you in, get you wet, get you gone. Certainly not enough to get you warm.

When he got rich, he dreamed of a place with two water heater tanks, so he could take a super-hot shower that lasted for an hour, each tank cycling, back and forth, as he absorbed heat like a lizard on a particularly good rock. He would come out of his awesome bathroom all pruned up, totally relaxed.

It was a hotel, so there were limits to how hot he could get the water. Still, it got hot enough. He climbed in and let the warmth leech into his bones.

After a few minutes, he opened his eyes and cast about for the complimentary shampoo thingee. There. A razor would be nice, about now. Good bristly stubble going. If he couldn't go home tomorrow, he would have to pick up a pack of disposables.

Could he go home?

If the bad buy knew about him, he knew about the restaurant. And he probably knew where Rick lived, all of four blocks away, in an old dingbat on 59ᵗʰ that was still cheap enough as the rest of the neighborhood got gentrified by yuppies.

Gotta get through tonight. Need sleep. Tomorrow will be here too soon.

Rick used up the whole shampoo bottle getting clean. It felt good to get off all the grime of the kitchen, overlain with muck and squelch from the Gardens. Sunday nights had gotten to be this kind of ritual when he got home. Quick shower. Couple of cigarettes. Something dumb on television until he unwound enough to actually crash. Sleep.

Rick really needed a cigarette. And a new lighter. And he couldn't smoke here anyway, so he'd have to wait until all his clothes were dry so he could walk down to a convenience store and buy more.

Yeah, he'd be grumpy by then.

The water was finally off. He dripped for a bit until he started to shiver. Grabbed a towel. Wow, nice towels. Rick couldn't remember the last time he'd felt a towel this soft. Might have to invest in some new ones, if they were going to be this nice.

Dry, he stepped out onto the little mat and looked at himself in the mirror. Five miles of bad gravel road stared back. Whatever.

Rick wrapped the towel around his waist and opened the bathroom door. He figured he could find something on the television to distract him for a while.

Rick's jaw dropped open.

He wasn't prepared for the distraction he found.

Laurie was back from her trip to the basement.

"Where's your shirt?" he asked blankly.

Laurie was sitting on the bed, checking something on her phone. Her boots were by the door. She had worn bright purple socks underneath. She still had on those second-skin jeans. Her black leather jacket hung open with nothing under it, teasing him with enough view of her tits that he had a hard time concentrating.

She was right. They were perfect. And if they were as fake as she said, the doc had done an amazing job.

She looked up at him quizzically, then glanced down at her own chest, before she speared him with a serious mien.

"My own shirt was almost as wet and dirty as your clothing," she replied calmly. "Do you find it inappropriate that I washed it as well?"

Rick blinked, tried to drag his eyes up to her face and hold them there. It wasn't easy. Oh, what the hell…

"It's not that," he said. "I just wasn't prepared to find you like this."

"Do you not find them engaging?" she said.

Rick was about to respond when she grabbed both sides of her jacket and pulled them open, like wings, and proudly displayed her breasts to him.

Rick goggled. They were very nice. Firm. Round. Pointed.

As he watched, the nipples seemed to harden into finer points, twin spears aimed at him. His brain turned to white noise.

What the hell was wrong with this chick? What the hell was wrong with him?

After a moment, she pulled the leather closed.

Rick felt a small moan escape his lips involuntarily as she did so.

"But," she said, "if you were prefer, I will keep them covered." She proceeded to zip the jacket up enough to cover things, even if it did seem to push her to a nice amount of cleavage threatening to spill over.

Rick's brain came back on line after a breath. He finally realized that Laurie had gotten them a king-sized bed, rather than a pair of smaller ones. And she had bunched up most of the pillows in the middle, like a queen on a throne.

As he watched, she powered her phone down and stuffed it into an inside pocket on the leather jacket, right where Rick's mind was at that moment. He could see where her full breast pressed it against the leather, a rectangle advertising how perfect her breasts were.

It wasn't fair. Not one bit.

She slid off the far side of the bed and gave him a tight smile. "The wash should be done," she said quietly. "I need to put everything in to dry, and when I come back, we can figure out what we will do next."

Rick watched that fantastic ass sashay to the door, open it, and disappear.

He collapsed onto the bed and tried to think.

Laurie stood outside the door and felt a human blush climb from her navel to the tips of her ears. Had she really just flashed her breasts at him?

She felt her breath catch. In two years as a pseudo-human and field agent, she had not gotten physically involved with anyone. Her own kind would have reacted with dismay or disgust at the suggestion after her transformation. And she had been busy with reconnaissance and operations. There had been no time to explore her human sexuality with another, even if she had found anyone interesting enough to experiment with.

And yet, here she was, acting like a schoolgirl with her first crush. Laurie supposed there was something to that as she tried to walk off the wave of emotion that threatened to drown her.

This body, designed to fit in with humans and to distract them with beauty and form, was technically a virgin. It had never mated with a human. And she had not been in any physical relationship in a long time. Not as long as Rick, but still, it had been many years, human time.

Was it the adrenalin rush of the moment that drew her to him? Or perhaps the fact that the entire *Collective* had trusted him with knowledge of their existence, and he had proven worthy?

Certainly, there was something to his smell that brought entirely unprofessional thoughts to her mind. She felt a burning need in places that had never felt burning, or need.

Was Rick the one to quench this sudden fire?

She had no answer. To even ask the question marked her apart from her kind.

She pushed off from the wall and drove herself to the stairs. The clothes would distract her for a while.

Hopefully Rick would asleep when she got back and she could avoid confronting this particular demon that had taken root in her stomach. It would be easier. She told herself that as she bounced down the stairs.

She didn't believe it for a moment.

Chapter 10

The old garage was just as quiet from the rear as it had been from the street. Detective Hall looked down, but there wasn't even trash around, in the kind of alley that was a magnet for that sort of thing. Weird.

So, old red-brick structure that had been extended at least twice, by two different owners, over the decades. The kind of place that had originally had two bays to work on a car, plus an office. Maybe it had been a gas station in the way early days a century ago.

What had been the back lot was now building. Storage had been added the first time, or maybe space for longer cars. Maybe ten extra feet. The second extension, later, had added another fifteen hundred square feet, but with those long skinny windows that were seven feet up and let in light, but didn't let anyone look in, unless they were standing on the trunk of a car.

Detective Hall could see a side door in the first construction, an old wood affair that was still around, but didn't look like it had been opened in years.

There was a back door as well. It looked metal and heavy, the kind you found in a movie theater exiting out onto the back parking lot.

A motion sensor light sat above it, with two big halogen bulbs pointed outwards. It was dark now, but it would absolutely light up the whole alley when it came on. Somebody inside couldn't see out back, unless there was a

CCTV that she couldn't see, but the lights coming on would alert them that something was going on.

Again, no dogs barking. Hall was willing to bet that there were almost no stray cats around as well. Just too quiet.

"Murray," she whispered, "have you seen enough?"

He grunted.

She waited.

"Unless you know of a crime, Murray," she continued, "there's not a lot we can do here except come back in the morning. Breaking and entering at the Locks and destruction of private property isn't enough to get a judge out of bed this late on a Sunday night."

"Yeah," he finally replied, "I know. Still, there's something here that's not right. I can't put my finger on it."

"I know how you feel," Hall said. "Tomorrow, we'll-…"

She paused as a car approached on the street out front and turned into the driveway.

She got just a quick glance at it. The car was a black Mercedes coupe. The really expensive type. The kind that didn't belong in a neighborhood like this.

Eleanora heard a garage door opener grinding the door up.

Murray turned to her with a quick, "Let's go," jogged up the side of the building, out of sight of the vehicle.

"What?" Hall said. "Shit." After a moment, she followed.

Murray was right. It was weird. And it just kept getting weirder.

Chapter 11

Laurie took a deep breath in the hall before she put the key in the lock. Half of her hoped that Rick's exhaustion had caught up with him, and she would find him deep asleep when she opened the door.

The other half was not so sure.

She adjusted the zipper on her jacket one last time. Just high enough to cover everything. Barely. If she didn't move suddenly. Or breathe too deep.

She opened the door as quietly as she could.

Rick was asleep on the bed, or at least dozing. His phone was on the nightstand. The pile of pillows had been divvied up into his and hers. He was under the covers, flat on his back, breathing regularly and deep.

She slipped inside the room and closed the door as quietly as she had opened it, watching him the entire time. He seemed lost in dream.

The clothes would take an hour to dry. Laurie's boots were still by the door where she had left them earlier. She pulled out her own phone, set an alarm, and placed it on the dresser before she quietly unzipped her jacket and hung it from the chair.

She unbuttoned her jeans, sat down in the chair, and carefully wriggled out of them, making as little noise as possible.

As she folded the denim and sat her jeans down, Laurie considered the gray boyshorts she was wearing and the purple socks. Had she any inkling the evening would turn out like this, she would have matched things better.

She shrugged, turned out the lamp, and slid carefully into bed on the her side.

Rick had left the bathroom light on, plus her own eyesight had been augmented, so she could see almost as well as with the lights up.

She pulled the covers down enough to see his body.

Her heart nearly stopped when Rick started to stir, but he just rolled onto his side, facing her, without ever waking.

She watched him breathe from a foot away. All the tension seemed to have bled out of his face. She could see where he had had lines and scowls earlier, only because he was completely relaxed now.

This was what he looked like when things were quiet and normal. She smiled at the thought.

One hand, almost of its own volition, reached out and touched his cheek. There was just enough stubble to feel, something else that marked him so different from all the males she had even been this close to, this nearly-intimate with.

It was a strange feeling. Larek would have found the hair off-putting, but Laurie found it subtly intoxicating. And he had a smell that seemed to find a spot deep in her brain and push a button that had never been pushed before, one she had never even known was there to push.

Her own breathing got very shallow as she considered the situation.

This form, this human, this thing called Laurie Bradley had never lain with a human in the biblical sense.

Oh, she had been designed to be able to do so, if the situation called for it. She knew she had been properly replumbed internally at the time she had been outwardly rebuilt.

Most of the parts fit the human design. She didn't have a hymen, or a uterus. But all the parts between those two worked just as well as they would for a normal woman. And they seemed to be working just fine right now.

She smiled at the memory of her early explorations. Scientists and doctors of *The Collective* had long since worked out the necessary physical and neuro-chemical changes necessary to make one of their own human enough to pass very close inspection. A very intimate inspection.

They had given her a long list of titles to watch as research and training. Human videos involving mating in an amazingly-wide variety of situations and methods. She had realized quickly that they were mostly all entertainment melodramas, human pornography, but they provided her all the cues she needed. Like a good actress, she had studied them and learned.

Her own explorations, in the privacy of her chambers, had been more interesting. Her new skin was much more sensitive to touch, all over, when aroused. She had breasts now, a whole new erogenous zone not quite exclusive to humans, but rare in *The Collective*. Playing with those had provided hours of entertainment.

The most interesting change, however, had been to expose part of her inner, sensitive, tissue as a small nodule externally, just above her new human vagina, what humans called a clitoris. Stimulated with simple touch, or a variety of tools, it was something her old kind would never understand.

It ached for touch right now.

She wanted to wake Rick up. She wanted to feel his hands on her body, exploring her in ways she had done, but no other else had ever been allowed.

She discovered need.

It was a hot, demanding bitch at the back of her mind, threatening to override the calm, rational parts of her psyche. She was flushed with sudden heat, overcome with sudden moisture.

It even had a smell, a musk, a signal that wakened brains, communicated desire.

She watched Rick's nose flair out at the smell. In his dream, he hummed a contended sound that played on her mind like fingers on a grand piano. She felt her nipples harden at the thought of him waking, finding her here.

Touching her.

Laurie fought the daemoness that threatened to overwhelm her. She was on a mission. Rick was an ally, not a plaything, even as much as she wanted to climb atop him and ride him like a pony.

She squeezed her hands into fists to keep from touching him more, or more intimately.

He stirred, possibly wakened by the overwhelming musk of her desire.

Her heart stopped at being found like this, close enough to touch, taking advantage of his helplessness in dream.

He cracked an eye open, pupil dilated at the dimness. She felt his eyes roam over her body like fingertips, caressing her intimate spots feather-light.

He returned from examining her human perfection and studied her face for a moment.

"Hi," he whispered.

"Hi," she whispered back, voice hoarse and husky, breathy and sharp.

She couldn't seem to help herself. She leaned in very close so she could smell him, taste him with her nose, draw a deep lungful of his smell into her soul.

"Are you sure about this?" he asked quietly.

"No," she said as she leaned in and kissed him lightly.

Laurie felt it turn into something deeper than a simple kiss.

She felt a hand come up and wrap around her shoulder, trace her back, grip her bottom, pull her towards him as she wriggled into his body.

The nerves in her back seemed to be on fire, as if he was tracing acid on her skin with each fingertip.

Need overwhelmed her careful analytical rationality. She slid close enough to press her breasts against him, to squish them against his chest, to wrap her own arm around him and feel the muscles play in his back.

Rick broke the kiss just long enough to lift her up and slide his other arm underneath her. She was engulfed in his arms now, legs tangled, breath shared, tongues dancing.

She felt him growing rigid, felt the pressure against her thigh. It seemed to center that burning need in her, even as one kiss turned into so many more.

It was good.

It wasn't enough.

Laurie leaned back to break the kiss. She fixed him with a stare.

"I need your help," she whispered simply.

With her whole body pressed against him, she felt the flinch that jolted him, felt him start to recoil.

"No," she said louder, "I want you. Here. Now. I want to feel you, to explore you, to have you. But I've never done this before, and I don't want to do it wrong. I want you to enjoy it too."

She pulled hard on his back, keeping him tight against her before he could move away.

"I need you to help me, to do this right," she concluded.

She could feel his breath catch as he watched her, unmoving.

The indecision nearly killed her.

Finally, touch.

Rick's hand pulled her closer. She felt him trace the muscles in her back down to her bottom. Felt him squeeze those muscles through the boyshorts, knead them, caress them. His eyes seemed to burn into her skin.

That hand continued down her leg, drawing it up and over his thigh until her heel hooked on his calf.

She had never realized how sensitive the backs of her thighs could be.

His hand came back up her hip, fingers on her side, the web on her ribs, his thumb tracing a line up the front. Touch traced her to the bottom of her breast as she laid there kissing his cheek and ear.

She stopped moving, willing his hand to move up, but afraid to move herself and spoil it.

Things turned to fire as he finally touched her nipple, running the rough part of his thumbprint over the sensitive skin like a cat's tongue. She felt it turn to diamond under his caress, with a jolt of heat that ran straight to her wet new human parts.

And then he leaned down and kissed it. Lightly. Softly. Warm and wet as his tongue made contact. Fire as he closed his lips around her nipple and tugged ever so lightly. She felt her fingernails dig into his skin.

"Rick," she whispered hoarsely, "I need to feel you inside me."

He let go of her nipple to lean back and look at her. She almost grabbed his head and pushed it back down.

"You aren't really human?" Rick seemed to be thinking just about as clearly as she was at this point.

Laurie responded by rolling onto her back and pulling him with her, until she had his weight pressing her into the mattress and could wrap both legs around him.

"I'm human enough," she said. "When they made me like this, they gave me human needs."

She pulled him down into a hot, warm kiss. She could feel his hardness rubbing against her in places that made it all the worse. There was a wet fire that threatened to drown her.

Rick leaned back from the kiss to look her in the eyes. She could see something vulnerable there. Loss, perhaps. Pain. It was a look much older than his physical years.

"Are you sure?" he asked her again.

Laurie responded by grinding her hips against him.

It helped, but it wasn't enough. She reached down to take his cock in her hands. She felt him ease his weight off of her some, but she kept him close with her heels.

The male sexual organ. She had seen them, read about them, watched them, but she had never held one. It felt right in her hand. And the fire in her mind would not let her go.

She caressed it like he had done her leg, her side, her nipple. Soft and warm, moving to engulf it and pull slowly. It felt like the most natural thing in the world to hold him.

She looked up. Rick's eyes were closed and his breath ragged. He seemed to breathe in rhythm with the movement of her hand, something no melodrama video had explained.

Laurie smiled to herself and leaned forward to wrap her own lips around one of his nipples, tugging and biting like she wanted him to do. His eyes flew open in surprise.

It was good. It was very good.

It was not enough.

Laurie pushed him back and to the side, off of her. He slid back, careful, as if he had done something wrong. She saw a caged animal look in those eyes.

Laurie quickly kissed him again and then fell back and wriggled out of her boyshorts.

She left the socks on. It was cool in the room, in spite of the heat emanating from her pores.

She tugged at his hand and pulled it to her breast.

He relaxed, leaned forward, palmed her flesh.

The fire inside notched up another level as he leaned close and kissed her neck, another erogenous zone she had never encountered before.

Humans had so many wonderful places to touch.

Laurie pulled his weight back onto her. She grabbed his cock and guided him forward blindly, trusting the programmed instincts to handle the task. She felt his weight center on her again, driving her down into the mattress as she found the right spot and aligned him to enter her.

It was a hot, wet fire that threatened to explode her mind.

She felt him press against her canal slowly, coaxing it open a little at a time with each slow thrust forward. The muscles there were unused to this level of stretching.

Her own kind never experienced the level of wetness that accompanied her current desire, but they did not have this kind of mating experience.

She felt her muscles open up like a flower greeting the morning dew, until at last she felt him fully enter her.

Laurie found another pleasure button when he bottomed out inside her, one that overwhelmed her mind. Each time he thrust, she felt that button depress and reset.

Her eyes threatened to roll back in her head as the waves of pleasure overwhelmed her. It was as if he dropped a rock into a still pond each time. Or hammered a giant bell with a mallet.

It went beyond sense, beyond comprehension.

Breathing grew sharp and loud.

She couldn't tell if it was hers or his.

It didn't matter.

They had fallen into a rhythm of grinding and groaning, her pulling him onto her with her powerful legs, him impaling her again and again.

Time seemed to stop, or go on forever. She couldn't tell anymore.

There was only need and fire.

And then the fire overwhelmed her. She felt it begin at her center, where he entered her, and expand outward like an explosion. In a moment, it overcame her. She stopped breathing for several heartbeats, and then exploded with a cry at her first orgasm.

She felt her moans become cries as it seemed to go on forever.

Atop her, Rick continued his rhythm.

His breath seemed to grow short as well. Ragged. Hoarse.

Laurie discovered that human females were capable of more than one orgasm at a time. It was a revelation that made the form worth taking all by itself. Her second orgasm was a continuation of the first, but at a higher plateau. The third threatened to completely overwhelm her enhanced heart.

Louder. Harder. Sharper. Her breath. Her moans. Her gasps.

Rick got caught up in her pleasure now. She felt his cock grow harder and thicker as it plunged inside her again and again. The increased pressure on her generated a fourth orgasm that had her clutching his back with her nails and driving her heels into his bottom with a cry.

That seemed to do something to Rick, as she heard his gasp and felt him suddenly erupt inside her, again and again and again. Their combined orgasm seemed to last for hours as she rode his pleasure, even as he rode her body.

An eternity passed.

The metronome of their love-making had ground down to quiet.

He was still inside her, but had ceased moving, except to gasp. She felt his heart racing, pounding, only gradually slowing. Her own heart syncopated.

She opened her eyes. Rick had collapsed atop her, his head above and to one side of hers. It was way too bright in there.

She kissed him once on the cheek.

"Thank you," she said. "I needed that. I'm sorry if I was a little greedy. It was unethical of me to take advantage of you that way."

The sound confused her for a moment, until she realized he was laughing.

It was an interesting experience, feeling his whole body shake, even while he was still inside her.

"Apology accepted," he smiled as he leaned back to look at her. He leaned in to kiss her, lightly, but with the promise of more passion.

She felt him shift his weight up and away. For a moment, she considered keeping him there, but she let him go. It left a hollowness in her, physical and metaphorical.

Rick collapsed beside her. A hand snaked out, grabbed hers, held it.

"It's been a very long for me," he said quietly. "And I don't ever remember anything like that. Thank you."

She laid there and let her heart slow. His hand in hers provided an anchor, let her close her eyes and wander vainly about as her entire brain rebooted and finally came back on line. The human theory of sexuality had been quite interesting.

The practice was unlike anything she had ever imagined.

Laurie let the human-programming instincts take over. She snuggled closer to him and pulled his hand up over her head so she could lay against his side and press as much of her body as possible against him. She felt his kiss on the top of her forehead as his hand gripped her back and pulled her even tighter.

Her free hand traced the black hairs on his chest, twirling them into sweat-drenched patterns. He gave off a smell that reminded her of her mother's baking, stimulating all the happy places in her mind.

"I promise to apologize again, several more times," she said quietly, unable to keep a grin off her face. "If you keep letting me take unethical advantage of you like that."

She felt him wrap both arms tight around her. "Deal," he said.

Whatever else he was going to say was interrupted by his phone, ringing madly on the nightstand.

"Who the hell's calling me at this hour?" he asked, grumpiness threatening to stain her bliss.

Chapter 12

Detective Hall slid to a halt next to her partner, her butt tight against the side of the building. She considered drawing her pistol. That might make things get entirely out of hand, so she stayed still. Murray hadn't drawn his, so he didn't think things had gone south.

Not yet, anyway.

The Mercedes drove into the garage with all the powerful purr of well-tuned German engineering.

She watched Murray slide forward enough to glance around the corner. Crazy-ass redneck boy from Yelm was in his element here. It was like a giant game of hide and seek.

Hall heard a muffled car door open. Murray's whole posture changed as he radiated tension. Still, he didn't draw, so she figured she didn't need to either.

A second car door opened.

A moment passed.

Detective Murray stepped around the corner and slipped into cop voice before she realized he was moving.

"Seattle Police," he announced, "what's going on here?"

Eleanora decided to move. Rather than stay close against the building, she stepped to her right and moved to walk around Murray.

A sound caught her attention.

Footsteps. Heavy ones. Sudden. Harsh.

Murray was suddenly flying backwards with a loud crack.

Detective Hall looked up into an equally surprised face, a man staring back at her, eyes wide, fist outstretched from where he had just punched her partner across the driveway.

Across the driveway?

Eleanora regretted not already having her service weapon in hand. Still, all those hours at the range, both with her partner, and at home, with her husband, paid off.

She flipped her hip to one side and back, clearing her jacket out of the way, just like the old cowboys did it in the movies. Her right hand snaked down, gripped, and tugged, clearing the weapon in one sudden flow of movement. The safety seemed to flip itself off.

Across the space, the stranger seemed to realize his mistake. Big men never considered a single woman to be a threat. He certainly hadn't.

Women with guns were a whole different creature. *Isn't that right, asshole?*

Hall had the weapon centered on his chest before he could move.

He moved anyway.

All that training took over.

Her first shot hit him dead center in the chest, close enough to leave powder burns. She would have felt really good about it, but it didn't stop him.

He closed the two steps almost too fast for her to realize it. She got off a second shot, high and left with the recoil from the first, about into the clavicle, maybe a touch lower.

That didn't stop him either.

Before she had time to do anything else, he was on her.

One hand brushed her pistol aside. The other was aimed at the side of her head.

Eleanora had just enough time to realize he was about to hit her with an open palm, rather than a closed fist.

What kind of shit slaps a woman?

Darkness.

Chapter 13

Tarquenic stood over the policewoman's unconscious form and let the surge of adrenalin burn itself out with a series of ragged gasps. That extra power, chemically-induced, always came as something of a surprise to someone who hadn't been born with it. Truly, it marked humans as a dangerous predator species.

His chest hurt. Tarquenic reached up under his shirt and peeled away two bullets where they had flattened themselves against the reinforced bones of his ribcage. The slugs were hot in his hand.

Both bullets seemed to be designed like some sort of circular buzz saw, an interesting step beyond old fashioned jacketed hollow points. Designed for maximum damage against a soft target. Say, a police officer shooting the average criminal deviant, rather than an alien cyborg specifically protected against that sort of damage.

He was pleased that she had not shot him with an armour piercing round. That might have gotten inside him and bounced around until it hit something critical and possibly killed him.

Again, proof that the Creator had placed him here for a sacred mission and would protect him.

Still, these were police officers from the vests they wore over their clothing. They were on his side, even if they didn't know it. He could not kill them like he had the common criminals.

And gunshots at night, even in a place like this, would draw attention.

No lights had come on yet.

They still might.

Tarquenic picked up the female and carefully laid her inside the garage before retrieving the male. He closed the garage door with a keen eye cast about.

Inside, Tarquenic considered his haul.

For a crusader on a mission to destroy criminal deviants, how had he managed to accumulate three innocents? Granted, two accidentally and a third for more devious purposes.

Still, he needed to do something quickly to cover his tracks.

Handcuffs would serve on the two police officers. Tarquenic quickly stripped both naked and placed them into the old office he used as storage. For extra security, he laid them down back to back on an old blanket and crossed the handcuffs through arms linked behind them, so one could not stand without the other doing the same, and neither could manage to get their arms in front of them.

He mentally thanked the human entertainer Houdini for the idea.

He left them there. Their clothing and firearms, he took with him and set on a shelf back in the garage. He would have to give some thought to this conundrum while he figured out how to escape the situation without having to kill his however-unknowing allies.

Both phones were crushed with a small maul to make sure they could not be traced here easily. Certainly, he could have located the devices fast enough. He assumed that the authorities could track them as well. When he had taken the other prisoner, the female, he had had to locate and disable a tracking device in her vehicle as well.

Had the police officers been expecting trouble, they would have handled the situation differently, so Tarquenic was certain that he had some time. Not days, but certainly hours. He could plan a little more carefully before he made his escape and left an anonymous message that would find them before too long. Still, he needed to get away safely, and do so quickly.

Mentally, he walked through the facility that he was currently using as a base. Everything he needed could be moved quickly enough.

Clothing was all generic and purchased with an eye towards keeping a low profile. Most of it could be abandoned here at no great loss. Everything else would fit into a pair of custom backpacks, one for his electronics, and one for tools and such related to his original mission of Search and Rescue operations in the North American Pacific Northwest.

He would have to drive to a new location, wherever it was. In this so-called modern era, air transportation in this culture involved magnetometer searches. Tarquenic smiled for a moment at the thought of an airport employee attempting to identify metal weapons on him, when most of his body was metal underneath the pseudo-skin.

His own ground transport was lost, obviously, probably for good if law enforcement officials had used it to locate this building that quickly. That meant that this identity was also compromised and should be abandoned.

He had the car belonging to the female prisoner, the bait, but that represented another problem. The two police officers had seen the car and could positively identify it. If he fled, he would need to be well away before they were freed, as there would ensue a massive and rather angry manhunt.

Couldn't these people realize he was trying to help them do their job?

Of course, if he eliminated all of the criminals, wouldn't that obviate the need for a police department to supervise them? Perhaps they were so focused in their pursuit of him because he represented a threat to their continued power.

Tarquenic had never considered the police function from that standpoint. Certainly it fit the mold for less-developed nations, where police officers were often a tool of state oppression, rather than protectors.

Had he misread the situation here? Fallen for some seductive human public relations gambit?

Kill them, leave them, or take them along? His day had suddenly gotten so much more complex.

It was not appropriate to simply them, not without more information about their true nature.

If he left them, he ran into physiological limitations. Humans could survive three days without water, generally. That might not be long enough to solve the problem with the agent of from *The Collective* and her human pet.

He had a dangerous foe. And her assistant had proven extremely competent.

Humans were just too dangerous in their current cultural matrix. It would take him several generations of selective breeding pressures to make an appreciable change in human civilization. Why did no one in *The Collective* understand this?

Fair enough. He would have to take his prisoners along with him when he fled. That would give him time to separate them and interrogate them properly, anyway. Obviously, there was much about criminal policing that he had not understood, or they would not have located him so quickly.

He needed to be better at this if he was going to make a career of killing criminals, after all. He had a tremendous amount of work ahead of him.

Chapter 14

Tarquenic contemplated the next phase of his sacred mission.

The human woman, the one called Bethany, sat in the only chair in the office, liberally secured with a human invention called a plastic zip-tie. Feet bound at the ankles. Knees linked and hobbled. Several fingers as well as both wrists. A piece of cloth served to muffle her cries for mercy.

She did not look like she would be crying for mercy. Cursing him, perhaps. She had a look of wild defiance and smoldering anger. The bruising on one side of her face, what humans called a "shiner," only served to accentuate the entire scenario.

He had left the woman clothed. She was not, after all, a combat-trained law enforcement official. Plus, he wished to communicate with her in a more civilized manner. Stripping her would only aggravate her ill will to levels from which there would be no recourse.

She watched him with the sort of glare that a rabbit might use when watching a hawk.

No, that wasn't right. She had the look of the hawk eyeing him as prey.

Fascinating. Absolutely out of character with the situation. Was this woman so sure she could escape her bindings and attack him? Injure him?

Truly, humans were a bizarre species, if every member had within them that level of violence, ready to be tapped at will. Perhaps his brother, and the other philosophers and politicians of the *Expunsion Tendency,* were right that violence was the only viable long-term solution. Simply annihilate the species and allow someone else to colonize such a useful, habitable planet instead.

It was a shame he would never be able to communicate such a message to his family members after this.

He dragged his attention back to the woman, the object of so much rage directed at him.

"I mean you no harm," he explained quietly, carefully, as one would with a barely-civilized species. "It is necessary that I use you to bring Larek and the human, Rick Pine, to place where I can eliminate them both."

Tarquenic listened to her mumbles for a few seconds. He lacked the necessary, human, empathy to understand what she was trying to ask, and had no interest in listening to her rage and screams. Instead, he continued on with his prepared speech.

"If all goes well," he continued, "after I kill them, I can free you and we can both get on with our lives. That would be the best, most ethical solution for everyone."

The look she gave him softened some. Perhaps she was a rational creature after all. Finding an ally, like Larek had done, was far too much to ask, but having the blood of no innocents on his soul would just reinforce the sacred validity of his charter.

After a moment, she stopped looking at him and focused on something beside him. He glanced around, fascinated at what could draw her attention away at a moment like this. He spied the little electrical personal defense device on the kitchen table.

Yes. Of course. The weapon had been entirely ineffective against him. He had read about humans who could ignore such a weapon, usually as a result of illicit narcotics that caused their normal nervous system to be immune to the shock.

Tarquenic walked over and picked it up. He thumbed the trigger and held it against his arm as he turned around. The current tickled, a bit.

"You were expecting to encounter a human," he said simply as he weapon continued to discharge.

Her eyes grew bigger as he watched her face.

"I am not," he said. "Human, that is. My nervous system, my entire neural net has been significantly modified to appear human, to an outsider, but I have also had a variety of upgrades and defensive systems added."

She tried to say something through the gag.

Tarquenic released the weapon and sat it back down on the table as he concentrated on her face. Human body language was so radically different from what he had been born with. They had no feathers to fan and semaphore with.

Finally, he gave up.

"I would like to remove the gag so we can converse like civilized beings confronted with a common problem, to which we can achieve a solution."

He watched her think for a second before he continued.

"This facility is entirely sound-proofed. Any noise you would make to bring assistance will fail. Instead, I will be forced to damage you again and consider you an enemy combatant. Will you behave yourself if I remove the cloth?"

She seemed to consider it. She finally nodded, the human gesture for assent.

Tarquenic moved around behind her where he could untie the piece of cloth and remove it from her mouth.

When a moment of silence passed, he stepped around in front of her and fixed her with an earnest stare.

"What are you?" she whispered, hoarse from the gag.

Tarquenic considered the possible range of answers.

"I cannot explain it to you," he said. "Such knowledge would mark you for destruction, either by myself or by my enemies. What you do not know cannot be held against you."

She blinked, apparently in surprise, at him.

"Larek?" she continued after a moment.

"The human female accompanying your cook," Tarquenic said simply. Any more would be too much. He hoped it would not be necessary to eliminate her as a threat to *The Collective*. Even now, the training of a lifetime would not let that knowledge get out.

She cocked her head at him in a strange way. More of the human subtext, the body language, that he had not fully understood.

"You mean Laurie?" she asked

He shrugged. That much body language had been programmed into him. "I do not know what cover identity name she is using now."

The woman studied him for a long moment. It was an uncomfortable stare, as if she could read the secrets and machines that made him up. He stared back blankly, wondering what other humanisms he was missing.

"You weren't born human, are you?" she whispered into the space between heartbeats.

Tarquenic found it was his turn to blink in surprise. All of the design work that had gone into him had been specifically incorporated to make him appear fully human to anything less than a medical scan. Had he been damaged in some way that made his mechanical parts visible?

Tarquenic concentrated for a moment and brought up his internal diagnostic display. It sat to one side of his field of vision, semi-transparent, in what humans of this age called a "Heads Up Display."

He noted the two wounds in his chest from the bullets that had not penetrated. Those had been successfully treated and sealed. The flesh would close over them in a week with little more than a faint scar. All other systems were nominal or better. His micro-reactor even had enough power to run for approximately seventeen years before it needed servicing at this point.

His disguise had not failed.

And yet…

Were humans truly possessed of some additional sense, some semi-conscious psychic ability previously undocumented? Many humans believed so, though none had been able to demonstrate it in a scientific manner. It remained in the realm of urban fantasy, or a reality subtly tinged with minor magic. Fiction.

Tarquenic considered the ethics of the situation. There was no safe response.

"If I were to answer that," he finally said, "it would mark you as dangerous. It would again set you up for destruction."

She nodded at him slightly. Confirmation, not affirmation. She even smiled a tiny, tight smile whose meaning eluded him.

"So," he concluded. "You understand? You will assist?"

"Oh, no," she said. "I understand you. And I will keep your secret, for now. But you are on you own with those two. I look forward to watching Rick kill you."

Tarquenic blinked again. Clearly, this human had badly misjudged the mechanical and physiological advantages he had over the human, Rick Pine. He was orders of magnitude stronger, faster, and more durable. Larek was the dangerous one, as she had been built to his levels of capability.

What could one human hope to achieve against his advantages?

Chapter 15

Detective Hall woke up with a bad hangover. The head-pounding like a bass-drum kind. The "oh, shit, what did I do?" body ache.

And she was naked. It must have been one hell of a party. She hadn't done anything that stupid in a very long time. Not since that one time with…

Then her brain engaged.

This was a mild concussion, not a hangover. She had been stripped naked and handcuffed, and left on a moldy purple blanket on the floor in an office of some sort.

The perp had knocked Murray out, then her. That much she remembered. She wriggled her fingers, felt warm skin against her fingers. She poked. Murray groaned. She poked him again.

"Ow, damn it," he muttered. "Cut it out."

"Murray, wake up."

At least the perp had left the light on. She was in an old office, probably inside the garage they had been staking out, from the looks of the furniture and the light fixture overhead. Early Seventies chic. Ugly as hell, last forever.

"El?" her partner finally said. "What happened?"

She took a deep breath. Nothing felt broken. Just an insane ringing in her ears. Someone was getting shot in the kneecap for this.

"You confronted the perp," she said. "He cold-cocked you. I shot him twice and didn't even slow him down. He knocked me silly. Here we are."

"El, I'm naked," he said.

"So am I." She took a deep breath as she said it.

"Oh, really?" she heard him chuckle.

"Get your mind out of the gutter, Murray," she barked at him.

They were partners, after all. She wasn't the least bit interested in fooling around on Dave. Plus, who would find a 44-year-old detective, twenty pounds overweight, sexy?

Of course, she was naked. Men got stupid around naked women. Just look at Dave.

"Can't help it, El," he laughed back. "I like `em smart, not twenty-year-old airheads."

"Deal with it, youngster," she said. He was all of seven years younger than her. And had never been married.

With some men, you drew the obvious conclusion. However, Murray liked women, he just didn't pursue them with the same single-mindedness he did bad guys and puzzles.

"How do we get out of this?"

"Well," he began, "if I had my shoes, I had a spare handcuff key wedged into the sole."

"Seriously?" she replied. "You read too much Ian Fleming."

"Guilty as charged," he said.

They lay there quiet for a few moments.

"I'm going to try to sit up," he said. "Give me as much slack as you can."

Eleanora leaned back as he moved.

It worked, sort of. He got up onto his butt where he could look around. She could see that much over her shoulder.

"Okay," he said, "your turn."

Hall moved her legs around and pushed down with her hand. She wasn't sure how much of her success was her, and how much was Murray pulling on her ribs, but she sat up as well. The view didn't improve much.

Definitely an office. Looked like the extension part of the building, rather than the original brick. It had that industrial eighties feel to it.

"Okay," she said, "now what?"

She felt him squirming around a bit, until he was more beside her than behind.

"Can you get your feet under you?" he asked. "I'd like to try to stand up and see if we can reach anything that might get us loose."

Eleanora smiled. Maybe those yoga classes had been worth it, after all.

She shifted her feet underneath her hips and felt him brace.

"One, two…"

The door burst open suddenly. The perp was standing there with a look that was either anguish or anger. It was hard to tell.

He held something in his right hand, extended it as he got closer.

Shit. Stun gun.

Metal cuffs made this a two-for-one. He hit her in the shoulder and held it there. She got the full charge.

She heard Murray cry out as well.

Darkness.

Chapter 16

Tarquenic stared at the human, Bethany, unable to answer her, what? Accusation? Conclusion? He could not be defeated by a mere human. Even when the cook had surprised him, he had managed to turn the tables and escape. Still, it would be good to establish circumstances where the ground favored him.

He could not use this facility as a base. Obviously, it had been compromised by the authorities. At some point, he should expect more police to come, especially once they realized that they had lost contact with the two officers who had come to this address.

He needed to be gone from here. And quickly.

Those police officers represented a problem.

He sighed. That, at least, transcended physiological boundaries between species.

It would be necessary to take them along. They knew too much. And could give a very good description of him, one that would tie his driver's license to the vehicle they had found.

The Mercedes was necessary as well. It had barely enough space in the trunk to place the two police officers, if he removed some things. The human female could ride in the passenger seat, bound and immobilized as well.

It would work.

"You could just walk away, you know."

For a moment, Tarquenic was confused. Then he realized that the female, Bethany, had continued to watch him while he worked out his tactics.

"No," he replied flatly, trying one last time to convey the importance of his mission to her. "The Creator has placed me here in order to cleanse this place, purge your species of the violent, the criminal, the insane. Larek and Rick are the only two who can interfere with this. They must be prevented. They must be destroyed."

She shrugged. "So now what?" she asked simply.

Tarquenic nodded to himself. "It will be a long drive," he said. "I will need to attend to your biological needs now, because there will not be time later."

"And the policemen? I saw the vests. I know the two more prisoners in that room are cops."

He felt the surge of rightness come over him. "They will be transported unconscious in the trunk of your vehicle."

He watched one of her eyebrows arch in a most peculiar manner. "In my little SL? That won't be fun."

"The alternative, human," he said distinctly, "would be to kill them. Any other outcome risks too much on the timing of things. I cannot leave that to chance."

Tarquenic could tell that she did not believe him, but he ran out of time to explain. A sound from the next room indicated that the two police officers were awake and communicating. They had recovered faster than he expect. Or the conversation with the female had taken longer than anticipated.

He grabbed the stun-gun device from the table and rushed into the room.

The two officers, a male and a female, had made it as far as to sit upright and were obviously attempting to do something.

He held the device against the closer officer, the female, grabbing her with his free hand to make sure neither could escape the electrical jolt. After several seconds, both had lost coherence. He tapped each on the back of the skull, hard enough to knock them unconscious, without, hopefully, doing any lasting damage.

Immediate flight was necessary.

With his augmented strength, Tarquenic lifted both and put them into the trunk of the black vehicle. To reduce the risk of damage, he reversed things so the two officers ended up face-to-face, to keep the soft parts of the human anatomy pressed inward. Additionally, he partially wrapped them up in a blanket to keep them relatively warm. The forecast was for temperature not significantly above freezing this morning.

Once that was handled, Tarquenic lifted Bethany carefully and carried her into the bathroom. The police were prisoners. The female was still potentially an ally, if he could find a way to communicate the righteousness of his mission to her. In the meantime, she must be treated well.

Then he carried her to the car and took care placing her inside. She did not resist when he zip-tied her in, nor when we hooked the seatbelt around her. She only mildly resisted when he wrapped a simple blindfold around her eyes. Nothing that would be obvious to another vehicle on the road, but enough to protect his secrecy.

And then, it was once around the building to grab his backpacks and put them at Bethany's feet, as well as to make sure he left no immediately incriminating evidence. The vests, clothing, identifications, and weapons, he left on a shelf.

They would do him no good. Eventually other authorities would arrive, and find the evidence. But there would be no blood.

Thus would the Creator judge him.

Tarquenic observed precious little traffic on the highway at two in the morning. Still, there was enough that he had to pay attention. At least, for now, he was going away from Seattle when many people were headed in. Once he got south of Lake Washington and headed up Interstate 405, he would have to deal with more gridlock, at least until he got to the exit that would take him to the far southeast.

He took great care with his driving. For one, the car's owner sat next to him. It would be unethical to damage her property maliciously. And, second, he was currently committing any number of felony crimes, doubly so with two captured police officers in the trunk.

To be pulled over now, for something so prosaic as exceeding the acceptable speed limit, would be to initiate death and mayhem on a scale previously unwelcome.

The exit that would take him into the Cascades was messy and overly-complicated, as were most of the highway on- and off-ramps he used regularly in this area.

What was it about this vicinity that caused such poor design concepts to be cast into concrete? Could the locals be impressed upon to do better work?

Tarquenic shrugged and navigated the vehicle out onto the smaller highway that followed the Cedar River upstream.

"Where in the world are we going?" Bethany asked suddenly.

She had been quiet for so long that Tarquenic had almost forgotten about her.

It was a voice that expected to be listened to, obeyed. Tarquenic blinked.

"I have established a facility well away from Seattle," he replied. "Larek and the cook can be lured there and destroyed with a minimal risk of collateral damage, or discovery. Afterwards, I can interrogate the two police officials and find out how much they know. With good outcomes, you will be able to sleep in your own bed tomorrow night and I will never bother you again."

"I see," came the response.

Tarquenic did not hear great enthusiasm for the plan. But, upon reflection, he could understand her reluctance to embrace this destiny. After all, it had taken him some years from first hearing the call to finally recognizing it as such.

"And why, exactly, won't they call the police?" she asked after a few moments. "What's to keep a SWAT team from arriving on your doorstep instead?"

Tarquenic smiled, though she could not see it. Still, there was triumph in his voice.

"She shares the same great secret as I do," he said. "To notify the authorities would be to compromise herself as much as me, perhaps more."

"So," Bethany drawled, "she's one of you? Is Rick safe?"

Rick? The cook? Of course he would be safe. Larek would have no reason to injure the human, especially if he had become her assistant. He knew what she was, after all. That question made no sense at all.

Tarquenic scowled sideways at his prisoner. What was she implying? Was this all some sort of grand and elaborate scheme to trap him? Was she in on the trap?

"Well?" she continued.

"Rick will be perfectly protected," Tarquenic offered.

The woman grunted in response. It did not sound convinced.

Tarquenic could offer no greater gravity to his own answer, not without explaining to this woman everything she did not already know. And that would, as he had said, mark her as someone who must be watched.

Humans could never know the truth about what was really out there.

Would they develop an inferiority complex and collapse of their own weight? Many in the *Collective* thought so.

After five years among them, Tarquenic was firmly convinced their response would be the exact opposite. Instead of retreating in fear, they would explode out in a fury. Human history had taught him as much. Huns, Goths, Danes, Mongols. Humans combined the worst elements of xenophobia with curiosity and willingness to endure great deprivation in pursuit of fanatical causes.

The Collective had had no word for mass fanaticism until they adopted the English word for it.

Tarquenic retreated to silence. The woman seemed mollified and did the same. The road hummed, ridges in the pavement providing a hypnotic interlude.

Chapter 17

Rick watched Laurie sit up and throw the blanket off of them. He hadn't realized she was still wearing her socks. The rest was kinda distracting. He hadn't been this close to an-otherwise naked woman in nearly a decade.

She handed him back the phone and slid out of bed. Rick followed.

"So what's the plan?" he asked.

She stood there for a moment, amazing naked perfection, completely oblivious to the effect she had on him.

"It would be unethical to ask you to join me," she said. "It will be dangerous."

"That's what you said about what we just did," he replied as he took her hand and held it. "And this is my business partner who's been kidnapped. I'm in."

She stepped back as he stood up. Not far, just enough that she was not pressed against his chest, staring up at him.

"Rick," she continued, "as much as I appreciate your sentiment, we are not supposed to involve humans in our affairs. And I've only known you for a little over five hours."

He smiled. "And look what we've accomplished in those five hours."

She blushed. It started below her nipples and ran all the way to the tips of her ears. Rick lost focus for a moment.

"Plus," he continued, "would you have survived in the park?"

"No," her face turned serious, "Tarquenic would have killed me. But that would have been the end of it. He would not have needed to kidnap your partner. And you would be home safe in bed right now."

"So what you're saying," he replied, "is that it is better to have a heavily-armed lunatic running around, as long as I am not personally discomforted?"

She screwed up her face for a second. "Put that way, it does not sound positive. But it is the ethical position. You are human. Why should you care what happens outside your immediate area?"

He stepped closer, made contact. "Because a wise man, a wise human, once said: *All that is necessary for evil to triumph is for good to do nothing to stop it.*"

She stepped forward, wrapped her arms around his waist. "That is not what Burke said, Rick," she said. "But thank you for taking up this cause."

She squeezed him once and stepped back.

"Now, I need to get dressed so I can get your clothes. My motorcycle is parked near your bistro. I can get there running in twelve minutes, and return here to get you."

"That's six miles away," he said, doing the math in his head. "Twelve minutes?"

She fixed him with a serious look. "That is correct. I can easily sustain thirty to thirty-four miles per hour on the flat terrain between here and Ballard."

Rick felt his butt land on the edge of the bed as his legs refused to hold him up.

"The fastest person in the world can sprint at just over twenty miles per, for maybe one hundred meters."

She stepped close again. He felt her hands wrap around the back of his head and pull it into the space between her wonderful breasts. He rested there and let the shock of her words kinda wash over him.

"Rick," she whispered down, "contrary to what you see, this form is not human. Parts, as you have seen, are a very good facsimile, but my legs are entirely mechanical underneath. Over a short distance, I can reach almost fifty miles per hour, before balance factors and response time issues intrude."

Rick wrapped his arms around her waist and turned his head sideways as it sunk in.

Alien.

Cyborg.

Monster?

Spy?

He breathed in her scent. Smelled good. Rich and clean, like a spring morning, overlain with the scent of their sex.

And no, he couldn't tell they weren't real.

Had it been all an act? A trap? A game?

Better, did it matter?

Ya know what? Not really.

Rick smiled. Be interesting to be introduced to her family for the holidays. His parents were both dead, mom from cigarettes and dad from booze. Neither had lived long enough to see him turn into a responsible adult. Probably would have shocked them ever worse than bringing home an alien girlfriend.

He chuckled to himself.

"Are you unwell?" she asked.

He hugged her tightly for a moment and leaned back. "Actually, I'm good, Laurie. Or Larek. What should I call you? What would you prefer?"

She was silent for a moment, looking down. "Laurie is my human name, Rick," she said, very quiet and very small. "Larek is the name I was born with, but that's not me anymore."

He stood and engulfed her in the sort of comforting hug she had given him. He could feel the pain in her hands, and the pounding of her heart against his chest. "Then you will be Laurie. You are as human as any woman I've known."

She kissed him once, lightly. "Thank you, Rick."

Her eyes got a very saucy look. "Or just as bizarre, crazy, and alien as any other woman you've known?"

"No comment," he smiled. He turned her and propelled her lightly towards the pile of clothing on the chair. "You get dressed. There's an asshole out there that needs to be taught some manners."

Chapter 18

Bethany continued to wrack her brain for ideas, but came up against a blank wall again and again. This thing, this creature in a man's shape, this wolf in sheep's clothing, wasn't right.

He moved wrong. He smelled wrong. He had not once so much as glanced down at her cleavage.

Bethany understood the power of good breasts. She used them frequently. Mostly for good.

In addition to yoga and jogging, she did push-ups every morning. She even had a workout shirt in her closet, given to her by one of the younger girls at the gym, that said *More push-ups = better boobs.*

There was power in that.

Every other man she had met in the last three years had noticed her chest. Some, like Rick, also took the time to notice her ass as well, hard and heart-shaped from several miles of walking every day. Hell, even her pastor had to concentrate not to try to look down her shirt, if she dressed a little too loose for church.

This *person* sitting beside her had barely noticed her at all.

It was almost offensive.

So he wasn't human. Okay. Did that mean Laurie wasn't either? This creature called her Larek constantly. Obviously, he knew something, but wasn't willing to say. And Laurie was apparently in on it.

She'd have to have a chat with that girl, when this was all done. Make sure she was good enough for Rick. No way in hell was some little alien floozy going to saunter in and ruin a good thing like that restaurant. She and Rick were too perfect of a team.

Now, how the hell to get out of this predicament? Bad guy has my phone. Cops guns were still back in Seattle. And I'm trussed up like a kinbaku model, although this wasn't done nearly as aesthetically pleasing. Clearly, he's an amateur at that, as well. No appreciation of art.

Still, we're driving somewhere. He said he had a base out in the woods. Just like a good horror story. Set a trap, with bait, like me, catch the hero. Well, fudge.

Did he really think he could just let her go when it was all done? Walk away with a polite "sorry for the interruption?"

Baby, you've got another thing coming.

Bethany sat and tried not to grind her teeth. He probably would have mistaken it for fear, not realizing that when she got a chance she was going to rip his throat out.

The transition to gravel perked Bethany up from her fugue. She knew they were someplace way the hell away from Seattle. Past that, she was a city girl.

They hadn't driven long enough to be approaching any of the passes, so they were still on the green side of the Cascades.

Still, they were here. Wherever *here* was.

The car stopped finally and her kidnapper removed the blindfold.

A gravel driveway with a metal gate that glistened in her car's ultra-bright high beams. She watched her captor climb out of the driver's side of her speedster and undo a padlock. He opened the gate, drove through, and closed it behind him.

Trees. Darkness. A little mist, barely enough to need the wipers. Heat from the defroster. Smell of wet Douglas fir. More gravel as he got in and started off again.

Welcome to the far end of beyond.

Bethany was pretty sure it was a driveway, but it went on for a long time, even moving slowly. She was glad he was taking care of her car. Not that it would save him if she got loose, but still.

The farmhouse was, somehow, just exactly what she was expecting it to be. Fifties rambler on a small rise, with a space cleared around it. Needed paint. A deer spooked from the bushes to one side and bounded off. A second, smaller one followed close behind.

Obviously, he didn't spend much time out here. Was this the secret villain lair?

She took a deep breath and forced herself to relax. She was still in no position to do anything, not tied up like this. She just had to keep her wits about her, and escape, while doing as much damage as possible to this punk in the process.

Or maybe do a lot of damage and then escape.

He parked her car near the front door and got out, leaving her alone. She couldn't have done anything, anyway, even so simple as to scratch her nose.

She watched this creature approach the front door. Motion sensor lights kicked on, blinding her, as he mounted the porch.

A few moments later, he opened her door, lifted her carefully, and carried her across the threshold like a groom on his way to the wedding bed.

Sweetie, I don't think so. If that's what you have in mind, be prepared for me to bite it off.

But he simply entered what had been the living room and deposited her in the only chair, a slightly over-stuffed affair covered with old fabric and surprisingly comfortable.

Obviously, this was where he did his thinking. There were no pictures on the walls, though she could see lighter spots in the paint where they had once hung. Similarly, the hardwood floor had faded and dark spots indicating where a sofa had once been, as well as a couple of book cases.

There were still some book-cases, but these held a remarkable variety of non-fiction books. Histories, biographies, hiking guides. *Dating advice? Astrology? Okay, that was the weird stuff.*

He returned a moment later and confirmed his alienness. In each arm, he held a person. A man and a woman. Unconscious. Naked. Handcuffed together. They looked a bit worse for the wear. That he carried both of them without strain confirmed her opinion. Neither of the officers was especially big, but he had over three hundred pounds in his arms and moved like he held kittens.

Yup, definitely not from around here.

She watched silently as he carried them down the hall to what was had probably been a kids bedroom, decades ago. She would have loved to have gotten up and watched. Hell, she would have loved to scratch her nose, right this second.

Deep breaths.

He finally returned and sat at a desk where she could barely turn her head far enough to watch what he was up to.

He glanced up and made eye contact. For a moment, she saw his soul, in that unguarded flicker before he shielded himself again. And then it was gone. But it had been there.

Nice words about a mission, sure. Under that? Oodles of rage. A whole torrent of it, just waiting.

He rose from the chair silently and approached her, that same calm, workmanlike half-smile on his face.

He bent down and put his hands on the arms of her chair. He was almost close enough to kiss her.

For a moment, seducing an alien killer crossed her mind.

If that's what it takes.

Then he straightened slightly. Enough to pick the chair, and her, completely off the ground, and rotate her ninety degrees to face the desk, before he sat the chair back down and returned to his desk.

Bethany blinked.

Oh.

He returned to his task. It seemed to involve her phone and some other device, something that looked like a moss-green river rock that chirped.

Apparently, it was an override, like the cops were supposed to be carrying these days. It beeped happily, and her phone was unlocked. She watched him explore the functions until he found what he wanted, and then held it to the side of his head.

Apparently, he was calling someone. With her phone. In the middle of the night.

"Hello, Rick," she heard him say after a few moments. "I have Bethany as my prisoner. If you wish for her to live, you and Larek will come to me. Give her the phone."

There was another pause.

"Yes," he said to an unheard question.

"Again, yes."

"I am located at…" Bethany heard him rattle off a long string of numbers. She guessed it was the latitude and longitude. There might have been an address in there as well. He was speaking too rapidly for her to follow.

"You have three hours. After that, I will kill my prisoners and vanish. If they do not mean anything to you, go back to sleep."

He hung up the phone abruptly. It sat in his hand, glowing.

Bethany watched him close his fist over the metal and plastic device and crush it like she might do an empty soda can. There was a brief spurt of smoke, then he placed the shattered remains of her phone on the desk.

He turned and studied her closely.

The moment dragged.

"We have some time," she heard him say. "Would you like some water?"

Chapter 19

Downtown was almost empty at this time of morning. In a way, it was fortunate that everything was happening on a Sunday night. Laurie could just imagine what the scene would have been like on a Saturday night/Sunday morning.

Seattle was the sort of city that never quite slept. There would be people around. Witnesses.

At least most would have discounted the site, marked it down to intoxication with alcohol or some other mind-altering substance. Nobody would have believed the truth.

Her electronic map had suggested she head up Elliott Ave to 15th as a straight shot where she could put on speed in the straightaway, cross the Ballard Bridge, cut over on Leary and climb up to Market Street. Passing two Hispanic men in an old pint-sized pickup truck had been fun. The looks on their faces had been hilarious.

It had broken her out of her thoughts, chasing each other around her head like a dog after his tail.

It was unethical to involve Rick. Time and again she considered that she the appropriate action would be to simply retrieve her motorcycle, hit the freeway, and go confront Tarquenic by herself. It was her job, not his. She could leave him there at the hotel and be gone out of his life in minutes.

And she would never feel his hands on her back again. Never taste his kiss.

Never smell him.

She was afraid this is what it felt like to be human. To need. To belong to a group, a tribe, a family. Rick obviously felt that way about Bethany. Not as a mate, but as a friend.

That was their power.

She understood that finally. Human friendship. Being willing to do crazy and extravagant things, because someone you trusted asked you to.

Had she ever had a friend?

Not like that. Not with that power over her emotions.

It was jarring. It was alien.

It was right.

The Collective, or at least parts of it responsible for putting her here, had not understood that. She hadn't, not until she had felt his emotions. His trust. His need.

He would never abandon Bethany.

She couldn't abandon him.

She had found a friend.

That was the most alien thing of all.

Laurie felt he great industrial beast growl and hum between her legs as she idled at the red light. It felt good to finally be in action.

She had never done something like this. This anticipation was an entirely new thing.

Sure, she had escorted field researchers, but Los Angeles was a tame and quiet place. The worst thing she had ever had happen there was the poor human boy who had apparently decided to mug her one night while she was walking around Sepulveda shopping.

He had even been polite about it. Walking up while she was standing in front of a Greek restaurant reading the menu and introducing himself as "the big scary black man." She so rarely carried cash these days that she'd been quite honest when she told him she had none.

Apparently she had done that wrong, as he had grabbed her arm and tried to drag her with him, presumably to a nearby alleyway where he could assail her. Possibly even sexually assault her. He had had the size for it, eighteen inches taller than her, much broader, and, had she been a human, nearly two hundred pounds heavier.

Not that she was going to tell him how much she really weighed. That sort of discussion would be un-ladylike. As was what happened immediately after he had tried to pull her along, failed, turned, and attempted to strike her with a closed fist.

Once she had learned to dance, both before and after getting her breasts upgraded, Laurie had taken to studying a number of Asian martial arts. LA was rife with dojos, and she did not have a proper day job to keep her busy, so it was a useful thing to study and practice to fill the days between missions.

Especially when you wanted to dump a bully on his ass with a set of cracked ribs and a broken hand.

Laurie grinned to herself under the full-face helmet and chuckled.

"What's so funny," Rick asked from behind.

Laurie blinked back to the present. His hands were laced together around her mid-section, carefully not roaming, although the jacket was heavy enough that he could not expect to feel much. His legs sat outside hers and his chest was pressed against her back, almost like they were spooning, fully clothed. On the back of her motorcycle. At an intersection. In the middle of the night.

She blushed again.

"Just thinking," she called back to him. "I've never done something like this before."

"You said that earlier," he replied.

Laurie realized humans could double-blush, or whatever it was that was happening to her.

"I meant going into combat," she said. "I've watched too many old movies. This feels like the cavalry about to come over the hill and chase away the bad guys."

She felt his arms tighten around her. "For me, it feels like being back in the army. Thought I was done with that sort of thing, you know? Just be a chef in a bistro and spend my days committing art in the kitchen."

Laurie turned a serious face to him. She even flipped up the shield so he could see her.

"You could always return to your home and leave these activities to me, Rick," she stated calmly. Not that she wanted him to, but it would unethical to not suggest the safe course to him.

She felt safer having him close, knowing his touch. His explanation of how Tarquenic had been defeated at the park. No, not defeated. Thwarted, for now. Yes. She could not have turned that situation to her advantage, not as quickly as Rick had.

She had not realized what it meant that he had also served with the United States military at a previous point. Considering his age and the amount of time he had spent in prison prior to opening his bistro, he must have enlisted when he was only eighteen, and perhaps only served for four years.

Still, that was an amazingly useful skill set to have, especially considering the current circumstances. If the other Search & Rescue operatives were like her, they could probably benefit from his experience and advice. She would have to remember to ask her superiors if he could be enlisted as a trainer.

"No," Rick said, intruding on her fugue, "Bethany is my partner and my friend. And I have other reasons for keeping you safe. Green light."

The non-sequitur jarred Laurie for a moment.

A hand unlocked from her waist and pointed at the street light. It had turned green without her processing the change.

Laurie flipped the face shield down, revved the engine, and started across the intersection to the on-ramp, waiting like an open mouth to swallow them whole.

Another blush crept up her ears as she considered Rick's words again.

Tarquenic, though? He was a dead man.

Chapter 20

etective Hall was just happy that Murray no longer ate as much sauerkraut as he used to.

The bastard who had captured them, kidnapped them, stuffed them in a trunk, and driven through wet and cold, he eventually had left them in a bedroom of some sort. Still naked. Still hand-cuffed together. Now with zip-ties around their ankles and cross-linked as well. There was no way they were going anywhere, unless it involved rolling over each other like a great big log like a kids cartoon.

Murray had gotten *whomped* again before the guy brought them in here, so he hadn't really seen much. She had played dead, just in case.

There had been a woman in a chair in the front room. Also a prisoner, from the amount of zip-ties involved, but at least she had her clothes on. Eleanora was willing to bet she was the owner of the sleek little sports car.

Hostage scene? Kidnap for ransom? What had they stumbled into?

She heard occasional voices through the closed door. One was definitely male, a quiet tenor. The other was the woman. It wasn't a conversation, the gaps were too long. It was more like one thinking of a question and asking the other, followed by answers or chatter of some sort.

Right now, she was more worried about Murray. He'd been out cold for a while. If she could have moved, she would have peeled an eyelid. She was guessing she'd see serious concussion signs going on. At least he was still breathing regularly and deep.

And if he was blowing his stinky breath in her face, it would just remind her to buy him a tin of breath mints occasionally. And to definitely get ones she liked. Not that she was going to kiss him, but if they ended up like this again, she would prefer a nicer smell.

And it would give her something to hassle him about at the Christmas party. At least Dave wasn't about to walk in and find them naked in bed.

She considered Murray's skinny frame. Not enough meat on his bones anyway.

Chapter 21

Rick looked at the map as he held Laurie's phone and spun it in his head. She had marked their destination on it before they set out, then left him to navigate. Now they were at a quiet intersection in the middle of nowhere on the side of the road.

Near as he could tell, they were about a mile away, around a couple of curves and maybe over a hill. He had had her pull over here, on the assumption that they needed to sneak up on the place, rather than come blaring in on a hot-rod rice-burner and let everyone know they had arrived.

Back in the Army days, those crazy bastards in the 173rd had taught him a few useful tricks about sneaking up on people. It was all flooding back now. He studied the map. Lives depended on it.

"So what did you have planned?" Laurie asked quietly.

"Well," Rick thought out loud, "he'll know when you get close. And if he has his little thingee set right, he might be looking for you farther out and spot you."

She nodded wordlessly.

"But it won't work on me," he continued. "I mean, it will, but you've got too many bears and elk and critters running around."

"That is essentially correct, Rick," she replied. "He will probably have motion sensors and perimeter warnings in place, but the indigenous fauna would generate too many false positives to be of much use in this situation."

Indigenous fauna? Really? Okay. Sure.

"So," he continued after a beat, "can you walk the bike close enough? We've got time. Then you sneak around back here." He pointed to what looked like an old forestry or logging road that crossed into the next little pocket valley over. "Then cross somewhere along this line. When you get close, text me a message, and we'll go from there."

"I see. Should I carry the beam weapon, or you?"

"I would like to handle it like we did before, Laurie," he said. "I'll have the gun and the fuzz-buster gadget and use it to target him. You can either flush him out, or swoop down on him if he comes for me. We make a pretty good team."

She smiled at him. After a moment, she leaned close and kissed him once, passionately. "Thank you," she whispered up at him. "We do."

She popped off the bike, flipped the kickstand up, and started to push it forward effortlessly. Rick had owned one like it, way back when, about fifty horsepower lighter and smaller. It had been a chore for him to push around.

She really wasn't human, was she?

What the holy hell had he gotten himself into, anyway?

Rick leaned against the bike and watched Laurie disappear back up the road. There was just enough city light and glare off the clouds that he could watch her move.

It really was a fantastic ass, even if she was approaching forty miles an hour as she vanished. He closed his eyes and rubbed them, shaking his head as he did so.

Okay, to work.

Rick took a deep breath and tried to settle his nerves. At least here it was cold and damp, and not dry desert heat. It should keep the flashbacks to the desert at bay. For a while.

A hundred yards up, he saw the gate across the roadway. It had the right number on it.

Rick spent five minutes studying it, but couldn't see if there were any cameras. He had to assume there were, so he hiked back a bit and climbed carefully through a barbed wire fence paralleling the gravel.

There were no other driveways around here, so the individual houses must be sitting on twenty acres or more. Maybe it was all forest land, or state. Hard to tell. Middle of nowhere.

Inside the property he was grateful for what little light there was. It felt like one of those really spooky kids' stories. Or maybe just the place to meet a headless horseman. Halloween hadn't been that long ago.

Rick crossed and moved inward a little through trees and brush, careful to not wander into the half-dead bramble of blackberries that reared up in front of him. From there, he found the gravel driveway and slid slowly along, ten feet back in the trees.

Hopefully there weren't any sleepy, grumpy bears around. He'd feel bad shooting one with the weird little blaster pistol thingee. Not that he wouldn't blast first and ask questions later. Crazy alien dude might be out here lurking for him.

He checked the scanner. No bad guys around.

At least this time he knew how to toggle it back and forth from scan to focus.

Ya know, good time to do just that.

Rick found a comfortable tree to lean against and pointed the gadget at where he thought the house would be, based on the map and the driveway.

Nope, nothing there.

A branch snapped. A low rumble of feet. The scanner pinged bright yellow and chirped happily.

Rick had just enough time and presence of mind to throw himself to the side as Tarquenic raced out of the darkness at him at high speed and slammed into the tree.

Chapter 22

Tarquenic checked the clock on the mantle. Dawn would not arrive for several more hours.

If Larek and the cook drove the normal speed limit, and perhaps a bit over, they should be getting close, possibly have already arrived by now. He glanced at the short-range detector module, but it remained blank. Still, some sixth sense niggled at the back of his head.

Shards, now I am beginning to think like a human as well. It is as if an infection had begun to fully transform me. How can they live like this?

The human woman, Bethany, appeared to have dozed off, as one would expect for a human who had been subject to so much stress and adrenalin.

Tarquenic rose silently and made his way down the hallway.

The floor here creaked, and the door needed oiling. The female police official was awake and glared at him. The male remained quiescent. That might not be good.

Tarquenic made his way to the side of the bed.

"Are you well?" he asked the woman quietly as he rolled the male over a bit so he could check him physically. The sign of serious concussion was to have non-responsive pupils, and unbalanced dilation. The male exhibited none of the symptoms, and his breathing was regular. Tarquenic did a quick visual inspection for other issues, but found none.

The woman was angry. Seething.

"We're police officers, buddy," she said quietly, firmly. "You are in a lot of trouble."

He fixed her with a stare for a moment to establish pack dominance. Being human was becoming a chore.

"I am aware of the former," he said, "which is why you are both still alive and why I have tried to keep your discomfort to a minimum until I am ready to move on. I would have left you at the other facility, but you might have been discovered too soon. Here, I will be able to depart in a few hours and I can place an anonymous call once I am away, so that you are subsequently found. Your partner has been injured, possibly I damaged a few of his ribs when I struck him, but his breathing is within acceptable parameters, so he should be fine with a few days of rest."

The woman's scowl turned to something approaching shock.

"What are you?" she rasped.

He considered her words. She lacked the fundamental theological training to comprehend his mission. Still, they were, after all, on the same side, even if she was bound by much stricter limitations in how she could respond to human criminality. She deserved an honest answer.

"I am the Angel of Wrath, human," he replied, mustering as much dignity as he could into his voice. "It is my mission to destroy the predators that haunt your cities, to help the rest of you prepare for a brighter future."

Her eyes got much larger and her mouth fell open. Perhaps she did understand. It would be nice if someone else could be made to hear the call, to understand the need to purify the humans so they could be made safe for galactic civilization.

Tarquenic pulled down a blanket to cover them, then left her there. He closed the door as quietly as he could. It was not worth the effort to fix at this point, since he would need to abandon this facility shortly as well.

Still, it was an opportunity. He could reinvent himself, perhaps come to grips with being human. Certainly get a better understanding of his mission and how to resolve it.

Out in the main room, Bethany still dozed.

He considered waking her for another conversation. She had seemed a bit more receptive as the evening had progressed. Perhaps she would accept his apology now.

He was about to say something when a light flashed on his desk.

Tarquenic had put great care into his sensors about this place. Something was moving out there was not a deer or elk or other ungulate creature. Possibly, it was a bear, but it was more likely to be human. A different light would have come on had that been Larek, so presumably it was the cook, scouting ahead of his master.

Tarquenic pulled the portable scanner from his pocket and let it search. *She* was not within range.

He smiled. He could take care of the cook now, and then take his time locating her. Perhaps he could even kill her organic parts carefully enough that he could salvage the mechanical components. It would be nice to have spare hardware for maintenance tasks.

His mission from the Creator was likely to take a very long time to complete.

He considered the beam pistol in his pocket, but rejected it almost immediately. It would be necessary to kill the cook silently if he wanted to draw Larek in. Perhaps he should even try to capture the human, like he had Bethany, to force Larek's hand.

He shook his head in disbelief. It was all so complicated, and yet humans seemed to spend an inordinate amount of time on such topics, considering the popular media entertainment options available. Further proof of how far he had to bring them along before they could be brought into *The Collective*.

Tarquenic checked the scanners one last time and then slipped silently to the back door of the old farmhouse.

He looked out through the glass in the door. The barn was back there, originally for previous owner's livestock before being modified, as well as a small land vehicle garage and machine tool shop he had adapted. Tarquenic flipped a light switch to turn off the motion sensor lights on the back of the house. No need to advertise to the human that he had left the building.

He slipped out into the darkness and moved laterally along the side of the building. The cook was approaching from near the driveway, on this side. He should be able to get quite close before he killed the human.

Chapter 23

Laurie squatted next to a tangle of what might have been roses at one point. She was not an expert on human botany, but she still knew better than to get close enough to get stuck by thorns.

She could just see the farm house through a gap between several out-buildings. The back was obviously some sort of motor pool area, graveled extensively and faced with large doors on one building she presumed was a garage and an old wooden barn. There was very little grass growing up in the quad.

Movement caught her eye.

As she watched, Tarquenic appeared at the back door, back lit by interior illumination. He looked out briefly, then emerged and moved across the back of the house to a side.

Quickly, she grabbed her phone and texted a warning to Rick, hoping that the message would get through. She knew his ringer was silenced, and trying to call him at this point would just give his position away.

Still, Rick had proven to be exceptionally competent at surviving extreme situations, something he attributed to his *time in the sandbox*. Presumably service in one of the wars that had been fought by this country over petroleum resources in southwest Asia. She could only hope he was equally resilient now.

However, with Tarquenic outside the building, she faced a conundrum. Should she go to Rick's assistance or rescue Bethany? Rick had warned that he would shoot without warning, expecting to run into Tarquenic at some point. Blundering about in the darkness would not be optimal. She had to trust his instincts.

Laurie rose from her crouch, looked at the corner where Tarquenic had vanished, and ran across the open area as quietly as her Docs would allow.

The building had been painted a mustard yellow color, once upon a time. Today, it was faded to the color of weak urine. The wood looked in need of refurbishment and painting as well, old fence posts and porch well-aged and possibly fading.

She stopped at the bottom of the steps and looked back to make sure Tarquenic had not circled around her.

Nothing.

Carefully, she put her weight on the outer edge of the second step and then boosted herself to the porch itself. The light beside the door did not come on, though she had expected it.

Apparently, Tarquenic was trying to be sneaky.

Hopefully, it would, to use the human term she liked, bite him in the ass.

She turned the door handle silently and slipped inside, pulling it shut behind her. For good measure, she locked it as well. It wouldn't keep him out, but he would have to make noise to gain entry, and thus provide her with warning.

She smiled. Rick's thinking was rubbing off on her. She would never have thought to do that, yesterday.

Okay, kitchen. Old. Cheap. Utilitarian. Tarquenic was obviously not a cook, or he would have made the place look nicer.

She wondered what Rick's kitchen looked like, considering his first love. Probably a work of industrial art. She looked forward to seeing it, and him in it.

Tomorrow.

Exits through the kitchen to the rest of the house. One to the dining room, one presumably to what humans would call the living room. She glanced into the dining room, but it was empty, so she moved to the other opening and peeked out.

Bethany.

Laurie stuck her head into the room. The woman appeared asleep.

Laurie crossed the distance in two strides and put her hand over Bethany's mouth.

Bethany came awake with a start. After a moment, she processed Laurie and smiled.

Laurie put her finger to her mouth for silence. She looked at the bonds holding the woman, and realized that she was tied up, but not down.

Speed was of the essence. She pulled Bethany up out of the big comfy chair, over her shoulder in a fireman's carry and effortlessly hauled her back to the kitchen.

Laurie knew a moment of irrational fear as she looked at the back door, but Tarquenic had not reappeared. She silently opened the door and peeked out both ways.

The coast was, as they say, clear.

Laurie took a step, stopped, and felt an evil grin creep over her face. She reached back and locked the door before pulling it close. Again, not enough to stop him, but probably enough to annoy him.

She raced across the gravel, holding her load as softly as she could. Bethany did not make a sound.

Back to the rose bush bramble.

Laurie flipped Bethany over carefully and sat her down on the ground. There wasn't a dry spot, but at least this was flat.

Examining the ties, Laurie fished in her pocket for a tiny folding utility knife, opened it, and cut the plastic ties holding the woman's wrists, arms and ankles.

She looked up to see Bethany staring closely at her. Bethany looked entirely too calm for the situation, but humans all handled stress in different ways.

"So," Bethany began conversationally, "just what species are you, anyway?"

Laurie blinked in surprise. How much had Tarquenic told her?

"That is a complicated question, Mrs. McGregor," she replied. "Perhaps an answer could wait until Rick and I have you successfully away from here?"

"Rick's with you?" Bethany asked sharply.

"He is," Laurie replied. "Right now, Tarquenic is hunting him. I took the opportunity to rescue you, but I must go to Rick's assistance. Please remain here for a few minutes until circulation is restored to your limbs. I will come back for you as soon as I am able. If all else fails, there is a road that direction," a quick point, "that will take you to other farm houses where you should be able to call for help."

Laurie rose, turned, and raced off without another word passed. Tarquenic was out there, and he was hunting Rick. She wouldn't allow anything to happen to Rick.

Chapter 24

Rick managed not to throw himself into the blackberry bramble. And he managed not to drop Laurie's scanner, or the gun, either. And he successfully avoided getting broken by the bad guy, who did manage to kill the tree.

Upside, lots of speed. He knew that from watching Laurie move.

Downside, zero maneuverability. *And trees can't dodge. They did shatter well. And fell over exceptionally loudly. And that looked like it hurt.*

Rick rolled over and pulled the trigger. He was getting the hang of the gun now. He just out of practice at firing snap shots from his back. He went wide again.

Not very wide. He hit the tree stump bad guy was laying half-across. It exploded like one of those big fireworks on the Fourth.

Rick discovered he was half-blind from the flash. On general principle he threw himself into a roll, farther away from the bramble.

He looked up to see the bad guy staggering rapidly towards him before he could stand up. Apparently Tarquenic had broken something. Not enough to stop him, but enough to slow him down.

Not enough though.

Rick tried to raise the pistol for another shot, but the guy swung a hand and knocked it away. Rick felt his right hand go numb and his brain went white for a second.

Before he could move, the guy picked him up off the ground and started to shake him.

Rick was surprised, then he remembered who he was dealing with. Or rather, what.

In prison, the first move in a fight like this was to kick the other guy in the balls. Laurie had said that she was built mostly human, except for certain bits down there. This punk was probably externally identical.

Any smart engineer wouldn't leave him so vulnerable to a swift shot.

Wouldn't they?

Rick punched him in the throat, instead. Hard to armor. Soft target. Exposed.

Apparently this guy had never been in a proper fight. Or never been to prison. Didn't know to protect those spots. *Crack.*

He dropped Rick with a gasp and started hacking for air.

Rick landed, and found his legs were too rubbery to hold him. He staggered a few steps to another tree and caught his balance.

He wasn't sure where the pistol had landed, so he looked for a big stick he could use on the guy. In his apartment, there was a big black baseball bat beside his bed, in case someone had decided to break in. He missed that comfortable hunk of hickory right now.

There. Close enough. Dead branch. Kinda heavy. Probably rotten. What the hell.

Rick pounced on the club and turned towards the punk.

The guy fixed him with a look of pure hatred and gasped for air.

Right now, Rick was so angry he was seeing red. He should have been asleep about six hours ago, and sleeping for another six. He let all the energy of the long weekend wash over him like fire.

Rick held the club in one hand like a batter waiting the pitch. He really wanted to pull a Babe Ruth and smack this asshole's head over the center field wall. They both took a step towards one another.

Rick snapped his left wrist forward with the swing, just like hammering a liner up the middle, as he closed the gap to the punk.

He felt it connect solidly, but the other guy got an arm up to protect himself. Instead of taking it up-side the head, the branch shattered over his left arm with a tremendous crack. It jarred the guy off-line, but not far enough.

With his next step, the man was on top of him and hit him like a running back hammering the gap. Rick had been a wide receiver in high school, not a linebacker. He felt the wind being driven from his chest by the impact.

He realized he was on his back, and the other guy atop him, before he could react. He tried a punch, but the guy ducked and Rick connected solidly with his forehead. Hopefully, he hadn't just broken his hand.

The guy snarled something at him and then slapped him, hard, across the side of the head.

Darkness.

Chapter 25

Laurie moved carefully through the damp underbrush. Southern California had an entirely different botanical signature, and far less moisture. Most of her experience was in the desert or High Sierras, where it was dry and cold or dry and hot.

She wasn't sure how she felt about rain.

Somewhere ahead of her, around the front of the house, she heard the sudden pop and sizzle of a beam weapon firing. Something exploded in a pyrotechnic dazzle that briefly lit the night.

She homed in on that part. Obviously, Rick and Tarquenic had found each other.

No other shots followed, so she was unsure if one or the other had succeeded. And she was too far away to rush blindly up to help. Rick might be too hyped up and shoot at movement. Or she might stumble into Tarquenic.

No, best to use stealth at this point. Rick had the gun and the portable scanner so he would see her. Plus, he was expecting her to be around back where she could rescue Bethany. She had done so, should she escape completely and come back for him? It was impossible to know what was the best course of action right now.

She would have to rely on guile and surprise. It was an interesting change from her years as a desk-bound analyst. At least the rainy mist had abated. It might be clear up enough to allow a few stars soon.

Rather than get too close to the farm house, Laurie moved well to her left, circling to keep a safe distance. Tarquenic would be able to scan her if she got too close, right now, and he would know she was unarmed if Rick had just fired a shot at him and missed.

Stealth and guile. But that would only get a girl so far.

Laurie stopped with a sudden thought.

She had fallen into the trap of thinking only of her own physical capabilities, or those technological assets she had brought with her. It seemed to a theme among her kind. Tarquenic was probably guilty of it as well.

But she was human now. She needed to take advantage of that. Humans were still very close to their origins as a tool-using species, capable of taking down much larger, much stronger creatures by using weapons and surprise. They had hunted mastodons and crocodiles. Apex predator species. And they were now the dominant apex species, at least on this planet.

Laurie froze. This was a farm. Tarquenic had purchased it and modified it to be his primary base away from the city. He would have his tools and equipment in the main building.

She smiled. What she needed would probably be in the barn. She pivoted on her heel and raced back into the darkness.

Being human was getting to be so much fun.

Laurie started with the smaller building. The larger one had the look of an equestrian facility, except that all the stall doors to the outside had been sealed up tight with wood. Next to it, the smaller building just felt like a workshop.

Horses confused her. They seemed to have moved to a very symbiotic relationship with humans. That had been useful in the past, when they provided a primary means of transportation. But today, they seemed to be oversized pets. But many humans kept them.

Horses didn't particularly like her. Probably because they were smart enough to realize she weighed more than she looked, and to take offense at being asked to carry a professional running back around. She smiled. The barn would be empty of horses for the same reason. Tarquenic would weigh as much as a defensive lineman.

Besides, it probably held Tarquenic's most important secrets. The size was about right.

The workshop building was much as she expected. This part of the country had undergone a significant spike on narcotics-fueled criminality over the last decade or two, as certain cold medicines were discovered to be easily converted into dangerous, addictive substances.

Addicts had taken to petty crime to sustain their addictions, with a rash of burglary and thefts and a flood of easily-sellable goods into pawnshops and online advertising.

Tarquenic had sealed the workshop, an obvious target, with a metal door frame and a heavy duty lock. It would keep the common tweaker at bay, although she could shatter the frame in with a couple of hearty kicks if necessary. She guessed that there was also some sort of intrusion system inside, probably a high-fidelity low-light camera. Especially if he was now hunting criminals down and executing them.

What she wanted, however, was actually on the outside of the building. Leaned up against the old wood, probably by the previous owner, and left there for however many years it had been that Tarquenic had owned the facility.

How long had he been assigned to this district? Five years? Eight? Long enough. Possibly too long, if nobody had noticed him going around the bend.

Laurie closed her hand on the old digging bar. Six feet of medium-quality steel bar-stock imported from India, shaped in a hexagonal pattern, tapering to a digging blade five inches across at one end and coming to a spire at the other.

This one had seen a great deal of use. The spike had apparently been spalled off more than once and re-sharpened to a rounded point with a grinding wheel. Probably one originally stored in the workshop beside her.

There was a very faint layer of rust visible in places on the bar. Apparently, the old owner had enameled the shaft at some point. That just meant that it was here and ready for her, all these years later.

She smiled and hefted the weight. Twenty-some pounds of medium-grade steel. Solid.

Most of the time, Laurie was glad that her original arms and hands had survived the transformation, even if having four fingers instead of three was a little strange at times. It was more of her old self to hold onto.

Right now, however, the same sorts of leg cybernetics in her arms would have been helpful. There was no way to throw this much weight accurately for any distance.

That would have been a lovely rude surprise for Tarquenic to discover, six feet of steel javelin stuck through him like a Celtic barbarian facing Roman legionaries in the open field.

Still, it was a tool. Humans used tools. She was human now. She would make do.

Another sneaky idea tapped her on the shoulder while she considered tools. She grinned. Humans were sneaky, evil bastards when they set their minds to it. This would be something they would approve of.

Laurie retired to the darkness and looked for a section of fencing to destroy.

Chapter 26

Tarquenic stood slowly. Something was wrong with both his left leg and his left arm and his balance was off.

Below him, the cook was unconscious, and would remain so for some time, given the force of impact to the cranium. Not that it mattered when he would wake up. This human knew too much. He could not be allowed to share that knowledge with others.

Tarquenic considered killing him here, just to be sure, but decided that he needed this human alive for now, to provide bait for Larek. Once she was taken care of, his mission could proceed without interruption. He might not even need to kill the other three humans at that point.

It would be one less stain on his soul when he finally met the Creator for Judgment.

Concentration brought the diagnostic programs live. The news was grim, but not insurmountable.

Had he been human, the blow to his left arm would have shattered both bones and left it limp at his side. As it was, the ceramic had suffered a grievous bruising and would require several days for the nanobots to repair. Already there was a long thin bruise running up the flesh that would have to be repaired first.

The leg bore similar trauma. The beam had not touched him, but the amount of energy liberated on the bole of the tree had caused a significant shockwave that had thrown him several feet. Joints had been jarred out of proper alignment and swelling was causing a significant degradation of capability.

As with the arm, repair systems would be able to fix everything in the space of a week. He would just need to adjust his diet to bring in more of the trace minerals and chemicals he would need. Until then, he dialed down the sensitivity of his pain receptors and got to work.

The cook was a dead weight, lifted and throw over his shoulder like a sack of potatoes.

He checked the portable scanner, but Larek was nowhere in the vicinity.

Tarquenic smiled. It was a sound tactical move, splitting up. The cook might have been able to get close enough to attack him without appearing on a sensor.

That just left Larek to be located now. If they had split up, would she be hiding out by the gate?

With a cold flush, Tarquenic remembered the ambush at the Locks. They had gotten him focused on the target he could locate, while the other had laid in wait. He had almost been destroyed.

Larek would not be waiting passively for her pet to report his mission successful. The prisoners were unguarded. They had drawn him away so they could assault the house.

Quickly, Tarquenic located the other scanner and Larek's pistol. He could not run while carrying the weight of the human, but if he had just lost his other prisoners, he needed to retain this one. After all, she could not get close without him detecting her, and she no longer had a beam weapon.

Tarquenic lurched into motion, back up the hill. Perhaps death was the only solution to everything at this point.

He found the back door of the facility locked. He had not done so when he exited, so he had proof that someone had been inside.

Were they still there?

He pulled the portable scanner out and did a general scan. No cyborgs within the normal scan range of 63 meters. Just in case, he set to a focused beam and scanned the interior of the facility. Perhaps she had found a way to mask her signature. This should find it.

Nothing.

His keys were inside, sitting on the desk. There was no time for subtle. He reared back and kicked the door frame as hard as he could, balanced on the damaged left leg.

It took three blows to shatter the doorframe, as one would expect with the amount of steel reinforcement he had added to it.

The racket was terrible. It would mark his location. There was nothing for it. She would know where he was, but he had a prisoner she valued. Especially if having the woman had drawn her here.

The kitchen was unchanged.

The woman was gone. As he had expected. He had fallen for the lure.

The two police officers were still tied up on the bed as he had left them. They knew nothing, and could be safely left here when he departed, none the wiser and none the worse for wear. It was a small victory on a night where so many things had gone wrong.

He returned to the main room and deposited the cook in the chair where the woman had previous been. He was going through zip-ties at a prodigious rate. He would need to invest in more substantial restraints if he continued down this path.

At least police officers came with their own.

The glass window in the back door shattered with a sound like the apocalypse descending.

Tarquenic exploded off of his chair, pistol in hand, and threw himself headlong to the floor at a spot where he could see someone approaching from either the dining room or directly from the kitchen.

His pistol sniffed at both doorways, but found no prey.

Several moments passed.

Nothing.

No sound. No movement.

Without lowering his eyes, Tarquenic located his portable scanner and pulled it from his pocket. He set it to general scan and held it up where he could see it and both approaches.

Nothing.

What in the name of the Creator had just happened?

He rose, slowly, carefully.

A peek into the kitchen revealed pocket devastation.

A rock had come through the window hard enough and fast enough to shatter it and send broken glass everywhere. It lay there in the middle of the floor, a little larger than his fist, mocking him.

It was not the act of a serious warrior engaged in a life and death struggle. This was juvenile delinquency.

How dare they mock his mission like this? He was trying to make this world a better place. These acts just reinforced the notion that this species was unfit for galactic commerce. His wrath would need to be terrible.

The other window, over the sink exploded.

Tarquenic fired a reflexive shot into a kitchen cabinet. The old dry wood began to smolder.

Damn it, now he was getting angry.

Tarquenic quickly grabbed a glass from the cabinet and filled it with water that he tossed on the scorched bits. That seemed to do the trick.

He would have to find a better solution after he had killed Larek, but he had time. After all, if she was reduced to throwing rocks at him from a distance, he had all the advantages.

He moved to the door and scowled out into the darkness.

I'm coming to kill you, Larek. Are you ready?

Chapter 27

Bethany smiled broadly to herself as she chucked the second hunk of granite through the window and scampered back into the darkness. If it hadn't been so dangerous, she would have giggled like a schoolgirl. Her, little miss strait-laced, up-standing, church-deaconess, pillar of society, pulling teenage pranks.

Not that anyone these days knew anything about her high school escapades. And Jill was still sworn to utter secrecy, thirty-something years later. Of course, the statute of limitations had long since expired, but still, there was the principle of the thing.

She ducked back behind the edge of the barn and quickly moved around to the far side. The second stone had drawn a shot from the man's blaster pistol, but it hadn't been outside.

Had he managed to shoot his own damned foot off? She could only wish. There were other parts of him she'd like to shoot off. Slowly. Painfully. And fingers and toes would be last.

She savored the taste of revenge.

Laurie had told her that his eyesight would be better than a normal humans at night. There was going to be a very long conversation with that woman after this, while Rick wasn't around. Woman to woman. Mother hen to son's new girlfriend. It ought to be interesting.

Bethany settled down and waited for the next step. Laurie had a delightfully wicked sense of humor about these things. The two of them might get into even more trouble, sometime, after all this silliness was resolved and Rick was safely back in his kitchen committing art.

She smiled.

Men.

Chapter 28

Laurie waited in the darkness. Against the lighter color of the house, she watched Bethany move close enough to heave a rock through the back window.

That ought to rattle him a little.

Thirty seconds later, the second rock went through the other window. That drew a shot from a beam pistol into a wall or something. Certainly, he hadn't been aiming at anything outside.

And Bethany had dark skin and black clothing. With the motion sensor light off, she would be invisible once she stopped moving. Not even Tarquenic would be able to spot her.

There.

A shadow at the door. And he had forgotten that the inside lights were on. If she'd had a gun right now, she could have ended this with a clean kill shot.

He had to know that. That was why he was being careless. He felt invulnerable. Hopefully, he would continue to feel invulnerable for a little while.

Laurie considered the rusting hulk of farm equipment she was hiding behind. It was big, and heavy, and green. Past that, she had no idea what it had been used for, but it certainly hadn't moved in a long time, perhaps decades.

It was slowly being engulfed by a thorn-berry bramble of some sort. That would just protect her all the better from incoming fire. The beam liberated all of its energy on impact, so it had no penetration.

Out here, that meant that it might not even get to the metal carcass until several shots had been wasted blasting away vines.

Time to rattle him some more.

Laurie held a smooth stone in one hand. It was slowly warming from her internal heat. It felt absolutely natural to step forward and heave the stone overhand, like a left fielder throwing out a runner at home. And left fielders did not have the advantage of her legs and back reinforcements to add power to the throw.

A black blur flashed through the night as Tarquenic stepped out onto the porch, looking for a target to kill.

At this range, he couldn't find her unless he took the time to do a slow scan, and even then he might miss her behind the mass of metal.

The rock missed hitting him in the face. But not by much. In fact, it was much closer than she expected. She might have actually gotten the runner at home with that toss. Maybe she should take up softball and play in a league. She did have a number of unfair advantages, after all.

The motion sensor housing and the light shattered under the impact. Which, on balance, was probably a good thing. It took away one more of Tarquenic's tools.

And it looked like it shocked the hell out of him, considering the shot he fired wildly into the ground. Gravel exploded from the heat, causing more noise and light.

Laurie smiled and reached deep inside for her inner Visigoth.

The next stone flew wider than she intended. Probably the extra adrenalin. It slammed into the side of the house and made the old wood ring like a bass drum.

Now to see if the old tractor was good enough. Laurie ducked down behind the big scraper thing with the spinning loom bits and leaned back so her voice would carry better.

"Tarquenic," she yelled, "are you ready to surrender yet?"

A flash of light and the familiar whip-crack behind her seemed to indicate an unwillingness on his part.

Sure enough. He could sort of detect her. At least well enough to aim in this direction. But he couldn't get to her from there. And the wet vines were going to do a reasonable job of protecting her for a bit.

Not long, but she didn't need long.

A second shot. Flash of light. Sizzle of cooking vegetation.

Huh. Hadn't even made it through to the cold metal hulk protecting her butt.

She wondered if the pistol had enough of a charge to actually burn through the metal before it went dead. Shame if he ran out of juice before she made him mad.

"Oh, come on, you alien fuckup," she called. Exasperation seemed to make the sound ring extra loud off all the facing walls in the quad. "Can't you do any better than that?"

Laurie peeked over the rim of old steel.

Yup. Looking right this way. Can't see anything.

He was trying to find her, eyeballs trying to pierce the gloom, scanner trying to penetrate the old tractor. It would have been hilarious if it wasn't so dangerous.

Maybe that's why humans are so unpredictable. This is kinda exciting.

Just for fun, Laurie chucked her third rock in the air. It didn't have any force behind it, squatted sideways like this. And wasn't intended to do anything more than make him jump again.

Of course, it hit him square in the chest.

Couldn't have done that again if I'd been planning. Maybe the Gods really are British. I'm having a black comedy kind of night, here.

She watched Tarquenic take careful aim and fire a shot. She ducked down, just in case.

This one made steel ring, so either he had found an opening, or had burned off all the vines to get to her. Only a matter of time now.

Either way, time to skedaddle.

Humans had such interesting vocabulary for the chase.

A second shot impacted, as fast as the pistol could cycle the charging circuits.

Good. He was mad now.

Laurie bolted as the second deep gong rang.

"Better luck, next time, punk," she yelled over her shoulder as she bolted.

There was a game trail here. She turned and raced down it, thankful that she was dealing with her own kind and not humans. Bullets would have passed right through the underbrush and killed her. He had to find a line of sight to shoot her.

Not tonight, asshole.

Chapter 29

Tarquenic cursed under his breath. He had already fired two shots in surprise tonight, one in the kitchen, another outside. It was entirely unprofessional behavior on his part.

When he captured that woman, he was going to tear her apart slowly. The feet would come off first. There were, after all, only four bolts holding them on in the first place.

Then perhaps he would shatter her hands. From her file, he knew that they were organic. That would make it amazingly painful. He would take his time killing her.

It might require days.

The back yard was dark. He glanced at the lighting system, but she had destroyed it with her first attack. There was nothing he could do for now to address it. There had never been a need.

Instead, he stepped down to the gravel. That would afford him more mobility. She had to be close, but the portable scanner was not locating her.

"Tarquenic," Larek's voice came out of the darkness, "are you ready to surrender yet?"

The echoes made it impossible to isolate her, although it seemed to come from ahead of him, back towards the overgrown fields.

He fired a shot in that direction, hoping the sudden light would catch her in the open. He remembered a dead combine at the edge of the field, slowly being eaten by blackberries.

A faint hash of a signal appeared on the scanner. Sure enough, she had taken refuge behind the tractor.

There. The beam impacted close by, but did not seem to have the penetration necessary to reach her.

"Oh, come on, you alien fuckup," Larek taunted him. "Can't you do any better than that?"

For a moment, she appeared on the scanner. For whatever reason, it was difficult to lock on to her with the scanner. Perhaps if he moved closer, he could switch to general scan and run her down.

The rock slamming into his injured arm was a terrible surprise.

Tarquenic went red with anger.

She was going to fight him with rocks? Fine. He would show her what a foolish idea it was to try to defeat him.

Tarquenic took careful aim and fired. He was rewarded by the sound of his beam impacting on raw metal. A giant bell filled the night with the sound of victory.

Tarquenic put a second shot into the same place as fast as the weapon would recycle. Another terrible gong.

The bell tolls for thee, Larek. Enjoy your time in hell.

He caught movement as she ran.

"Better luck, next time, punk," floated back over her shoulder from the darkness.

Tarquenic pulled the trigger.

Nothing happened.

Recycle. Of course, she is as aware of the limitations of the weapon as I am. Still, I know where she is now. And I can find her in the darkness. It is only a matter of time.

Tarquenic flipped his portable scanner to general mode and pushed off with his left foot. The damage was not so bad that he could not run her down.

He had justice and destiny on his side, after all.

Plus, he had long since memorized the terrain in the vicinity, just in case he needed to escape quickly. She would take to the game trail, down and across the field, until she came out on the forestry road.

Very well, he could go straight, run across the field, and cut her off.

He smiled and started to sprint.

Sudden movement out of the corner of his eye caught him off-stride and off-balance.

Bethany…

Chapter 30

Bethany sat perfectly still by the side of the barn and watched the two aliens engage in a war of words and blaster fire across the driveway. Laurie punctuated her discussion with large river rocks.

Bethany would have preferred something with a little more kick. When she got home, she was absolutely going to get her concealed pistol license and learn to shoot effectively, especially if she was going to be dealing with weirdoes like this. Rick better not have too many alien friends.

She did have to give them credit, though. Those nasty little blaster pistols packed one hell of a wallop. She would have been more concerned if Laurie hadn't explained how little penetration they had. All flash and no bang.

Kinda like how Jill's first husband had turned out.

Bethany flushed and suppressed a snort. She wasn't supposed to say those sorts of things. Jill was her best friend, after all. And her second husband, Brad, was much better for her. The kind that left a happy smile on his woman.

Right now, the taunting was doing the trick. She watched the monster fire several shots that only served to kill the old tractor further dead. The gentleman kidnapper seemed to be close to losing his cool.

Right on schedule. Bethany took a deep breath as the man started to move.

Laurie had warned him that he would be able to move much faster than a human. She flashed back to her childhood, and her favorite television show about a secret agent with mechanical parts. This one wasn't nearly as good looking.

She counted the steps as he moved, found his rhythm.

Right about now…

Bethany pulled suddenly on the metal pry bar Laurie had found, pushed her weight into it. One end of the bar was jammed in the ground, to act as a lever. Laurie had tied barbed wire around the middle, and stretched the rest of the wire across the gap to a post across the quad.

It had been slack. Now it was at knee level. They had both hoped that it would be strong enough to hold when he ran into it.

The impact jarred Bethany, knocked her backwards. She staggered several steps, would have fallen if she hadn't been expecting it. The wire went slack as she stumbled.

She turned and lifted the bar like a spear, prepared to have to defend herself. They had had no idea if it would work, and if it didn't, what they would do next.

She found him face down in about two hundred yards of barbed wire. It was like watching a man fight a giant squid. More flashbacks to Saturday morning television.

The wires wrapped around him and dug in tighter as he squirmed. Bethany smiled as she watched this smug asshole go down into the quicksand of mud and barbs.

She considered the big metal bar. It had a spike on one end. She stepped closer.

The gentleman kidnapper managed to roll onto his back as she approached.

The look of utter surprise on his face almost made everything else she had gone through tonight worth it.

Almost.

He still had this coming.

She reared back and put all of her yoga, running, and weights into it. Both hands held onto the bar as she slammed it down into the center of his chest, visions of vampires and wooden spikes dancing in her head.

The crunch was rewarding. Teach this asshole, and all the rest, not to mess around with humans.

Bethany took a step back to regard her handiwork.

And blinked in shock.

He was still alive.

And still angry.

And carrying the pistol.

And pointing it at her.

He snarled something in a language she didn't not understand and pulled the trigger.

Laurie saved her life with a flying tackle out of nowhere, or she would have been shot in the face.

Before Bethany could grasp what was going on, Laurie was up and gone.

Bethany got to one elbow and saw Laurie astride the man, riding him like a woman would ride a man, except she was holding the pistol away from her with one hand and punching the man with the other. He managed one wild shot as she struck him.

The blows sounded like hammers on anvils. One. Two. Three.

Finally, the man relaxed and rolled back, unconscious.

She watched Laurie rip the pistol from his hand and stand up.

Laurie walked close and pulled Bethany to her feet and then back several yards.

"Cover your eyes," Laurie growled.

"Huh?" was about as intellectual as she could manage.

Laurie physically reached out and placed one hand across her face.

Bethany heard the little blaster pistol snap once, followed by a dull secondary kind of thump.

Laurie let her see again.

The gentleman kidnapper had been blown to…pieces. The shot seemed to have been centered about on his belly button. He had a scorched, melted look to him.

The legs really were mechanical. She could see the shiny metal pieces sticking out of the bottom of his hips. The ribs were also exposed, but there was precious little blood. And the body smoked slightly.

He smelled kind of like a jerked turkey recipe she had tried once. That had ended badly as well.

"Are you okay?" Laurie was asking her.

Bethany shook her head to clear it.

"I am, but we have a bigger problem," she replied, pointing.

The farm house was on fire.

Chapter 31

Laurie's heart sank as she turned.

Tarquenic's last wild shot had apparently done some damage after all. The dining room wall had been kicked in by a giant mule, or a runaway semi, and the edges were furiously burning now.

"Rick's in there," she said, "I've got to get him out."

Bethany's hand on her arm stopped her.

"It's not just Rick," she replied, "there are also two cops in the back bedroom. We have to save them too."

Laurie considered her options. "How much do they know?"

She watched Bethany think.

"Nothing important," the woman said. "I mean, yes, I've been kidnapped, they're prisoners, and the bad guy is dead or escaped, but they don't know about you or Rick, I don't think."

"It is entirely unethical of me to ask this," Laurie said quietly, "but I require your assistance."

She pulled Bethany after her as she jogged towards the building.

"If you escaped, and fought the attacker, and he fled after setting fire to the building, most of the evidence will be destroyed and Rick and I can flee ourselves.

She was pulled up short when Bethany stopped moving. The woman was far more solid than she appeared.

"And just, what, pray tell, do we do about that?"

Bethany pointed at Tarquenic's corpse, slowly cooling as the reactors went off line and systems failed.

Laurie considered and discarded a number of trains of thought. She would have to settle for the simple truth and hope.

"Bethany," she said, "I have to invite you in on one of the greatest secrets there is. You will have to swear to tell nobody. Rick knows some of the truth, but not as much as you do, right now. Can I trust you? If this gets out, all of your lives are at peril."

She watched the woman scowl at her. Finally she nodded.

"Later, we will have a discussion," Bethany said with gravity. "Just us girls. Are we clear?"

Laurie let out a breath she had not realized she had been holding.

"Very much so, Bethany. Thank you."

Laurie raced the last few steps to the back door, Bethany in close pursuit.

The fire was bad outside, but the smoke indoors was less awful that it could have been. Her own lungs were better able to handle the mess. She could only address her part and hope that Bethany was up to the task.

Rick was awake in the same chair where Bethany had been held. Laurie covered his mouth to silence him as she flipped open her knife and cut the plastic ties quickly. He was up without a word and embraced them both in a giant hug.

Laurie could not put into words how good that felt.

Instead, she handed the knife to Bethany.

"We are going out the back-door," she whispered. "Make sure you exit out the front and get well away from the house, but not too far. The fire department is likely going to respond soon and we will escape in the chaos."

She blinked as Bethany took the knife from her and kissed her on the cheek with a quick, "You keep him safe, Laurie."

And then Bethany was gone, down the hallway, calling out.

Laurie grabbed Rick's hand and pulled him after her. The fire was worse now, close to engulfing the entire dining room and starting on the kitchen as dessert. She plunged through the smoke until they emerged out the back patio.

Down two steps and across, she found Tarquenic still dead and shattered. She knew a moment of sadness that he could not have been taken alive. She was sure that experts in *The Collective* could have repaired whatever damage had been done that turned him so far away from his roots.

"So he's dead," Rick said quietly.

She just nodded, unwilling to put her feelings into words. Not yet.

"Your bike is the other way. Cops will be here soon," he continued. "How do we escape?"

She turned to him solemnly.

He sobered under her gaze.

"The fire will destroy most of the evidence of Tarquenic's existence," she said slowly, "But this was his primary base. There is something else we will need to do, first."

Rick's silence was reward enough. To know that he trusted her was worth so much.

She picked up the metal pry bar and walked to the big barn. All of the stall doors had been sealed up. That had been the clue she needed earlier. Now, it didn't matter if alarms went off.

Laurie wedged the bar into the side of the door with the hinges and leaned all of her strength and weight into it. Tarquenic would have reinforced the lock, but probably forgotten about the rest of the frame.

After all, who else was strong enough to rip a door off its hinges like this?

Rick's face was utter shock as the doorframe shattered.

"Wow," he said, "remind me regularly how amazing you are."

She reached out a hand, closed it on his jacket, and pulled him close. She kissed him fiercely once. "I intend to," she whispered.

She dropped the bar and grabbed the door, pulling it out of her way, even still attached by the lock.

She had to take a deep breath and steel herself for what came next. This would violate every tenet of her training. If they hadn't already been going to fire her before this, what happened next would be the icing on the cake.

She paused and took Rick's hand. She gave it a squeeze.

He squeezed back.

Laurie stepped into the dimness, back lit by the burning farm house.

It was just as she had suspected.

The barn had been largely hollowed out. Inside, under a cheap blue tarp, was a ship. Tarquenic's ship. Tarquenic's starship.

She pulled the tarp to one side to reveal the greatest mystery yet. She knew Rick had seen a starship before, but never this close. And it was only going to get worse.

"Oh, shit," he whispered, never letting go of the death-grip on her hand. She pulled him with her.

"This cannot fall into human hands," she said simply. "It is how we will escape. Bethany and the police officers cannot know it exists. When we leave, we must burn everything."

They wouldn't have long. Hopefully, Tarquenic had followed standard protocols in maintaining the vessel and preparing the building to be destroyed in an emergency. She felt tears of emotion threaten to overwhelm her.

If she had just stopped the worst villain in *The Collective* in a century, why did she feel like such a failure?

Laurie entered the emergency code into the keypad next to the main hatch. It opened immediately.

So far, so good.

"We need to take the evidence with us," she said.

Rick turned and jogged out of the barn. "On it," he called quietly.

As she exited the barn, Rick entered, carrying one of Tarquenic's legs and the pistol, which he handed to her.

"Where do you want bits and pieces?" he inquired with a smile.

"Inside the ship, turn left, aft, and head all the way back, there is a cargo bay," she said. "We will stow my bike there as well when we retrieve it."

"On the way," was all he said.

Truly, he trusted her. It was a wonderful feeling.

Chapter 32

Rick sat shotgun in the little starship and tried not to pee himself in excitement as Laurie finished a quick pre-flight and lifted up to hover a few feet off of the ground.

It was one thing to talk about intergalactic mermaids, and ray guns, and aliens.

He was actually sitting in a starship.

Granted, it wasn't much bigger than an RV inside, and laid out about the same way, but it was flying. FLYING!!!

They crossed south of the burning farmhouse and the now-equally-burning barn and landed on the road just long enough for him to push the bike up the landing ramp and kick-stand-it next to the dead robot guy's various bits and pieces.

As they cleared the trees and headed north, he could see flashing lights approaching. Bethany and two naked cops had made it out of the house and down the driveway safe, according to the little screen, so things weren't all that bad.

A thought struck him. The kind that hurt. That meant it was a good idea. He hated listening to the good ideas.

"We're going to need an alibi," he said.

She sat puzzled for a few moments.

"Why?" she replied finally.

"Well," he counted in his head, "there's the gunfight in the Gardens. And someone kidnapped Bethany and hauled her first to SODO and then to east bumfuck. Two cops got snagged along the way, and beaten to hell. The bad guy has to get away, so he's still out there, and all the evidence burned in a fire."

She turned a quizzical look at him. "Why will we need an alibi, then?"

He shrugged. "We don't," he considered his history with alibis, good and bad. "I do. You don't technically exist, yet."

"I don't?" Laurie looked at him confused.

"Yup. If a new girl shows up in my life at the same time, the cops will think jealous ex-boyfriend and start asking a lot of questions. Dangerous questions. Which they're gonna do anyway. I need to play dumb. And have an alibi they can't dispute."

"Oh," she said carefully, "what did you have in mind?"

"There's somebody else who knows about you. I need to call him."

Rick pulled out his badly abused phone and unlocked it.

"You mean Deputy Gustav Harcourt," she said, "who is Bethany Harcourt-McGregor's brother."

"Yeah," Rick said vaguely.

"I had considered contacting him directly, originally," she told him, "but decided that his law enforcement background might jeopardize his loyalties. Do you think it is wise to bring him in to this situation now?"

Rick smiled. "Absolutely, Laurie. You see, they'll believe whatever bullshit story he gives them. He's a cop, after all."

"I see," came the response. Her look was not so confident.

He dialed.

It took a number of rings before he heard the gravelly bass voice in his ear.

"This better be good, Pine," Gustav growled, "it's five in the morning on a Monday and I have to go to work in a few hours."

"I need you to call in sick and badly hung-over, Gustav," he said simply. "And I need you to drive down to my apartment in Ballard right now. I'll meet you there when you arrive, and fix you breakfast."

"What the hell's going on, jailbird? What happened?"

Rick considered his words carefully. This was about to get tricky.

"So you remember that lovely lady you and I gave a swimming lesson to? " he said vaguely, "the one who stole my concert t-shirt when she left? Friends of hers happened."

"I see," the man said slowly. "And Bethany can't provide you a good enough alibi?"

"She's involved, Gustav. She's safe, she's fine, but the shit is about to get really weird and I need your help."

"I'm on my way, Pine."

And the phone went dead.

Epilogue

From his spot in the kitchen, Rick watched the evening wind down.

It had only been two days. Thank God they weren't even open on Mondays and always stayed closed Tuesday until dinner.

Bethany was at her usual place behind the bar, doing that thing in the cream of her latte to make a fern leaf. She looked calm, and everyone was giving her space tonight, afraid she might be too fragile to carry on, after all that had happened.

Rick suppressed a snort. Chewing nails angry was probably a better description of her current mood, but nobody was supposed to know that. If they did, they might start asking awkward questions.

He looked around the mess of his kitchen and sighed to himself. Tonight had been adequate. Not his worst night. Certainly not his best.

At least it was late. They could close the doors and call it a day shortly.

Behind him, Tonio had the dishwasher going and was almost ready to go home himself. Out front, Gwen cleared the coffee mugs from the last table. All night, Rick had watched her deliver plates with her usual humor, purple and lemon hair bobbing as she walked.

Flotsam's primary waitress knew the least about what had happened to Bethany, so she was certainly the most calm. And she was a stone-pro. That always helped.

Rick leaned against the wall to take some of the weight off, and so he could get a good view of the front table, the last one occupied at this hour. The smile he got back was the most reassuring thing he knew today.

Facing him, smiling at him from up there, was Deputy Sergeant Gustav Harcourt, in full uniform. Six and a half feet of former defensive end with a badge, a gun, and a snarl like he could take on the world. He might. The lighting in the bistro almost made his skin appear coal-colored.

Regulars who knew Gustav, and there were many, had been concerned about the look on his face when they came in, himself angry enough to chew nails, but a quick explanation had turned it all around. Everyone had been most accommodating when they found out Bethany had actually been kidnapped at gunpoint and rescued by the cops.

Well, sort of.

Close enough.

Gustav's dinner companions had been the most jumpy tonight, but they had a good excuse.

Rick had only been introduced to Detectives Hall and Murray tonight. The other person was their boss, a Detective Lieutenant whose name he had missed when they came in.

Bethany had apparently spent the whole ride to the hospital talking to them, spinning yarns and adjusting perceptions to fit the story she wanted them to tell.

Rick had once had to look up the term raconteur. That was Bethany to a T.

Both of the cops looked pretty good after their ordeal, although Rick made it a point not to spend too much time around cops these days, Gustav excluded.

He was family.

The rest? Nope, too much time in the joint. Professional paranoia. Never going back.

He could hear Bethany now, insisting that dinner was on the house, even as the cops were putting money on the table and arguing with her about it. Four on one? Even with Gustav on the cop's side, it was probably even.

And then, everybody was standing. Rick took that as his cue to come out from behind the kitchen bar and play professional host. Bethany didn't need the help, but he needed to play depressingly normal and concerned.

After all, there was still a kidnapper out there and he had gotten away clean. Right?

Rick swallowed his smile and shifted to hang-dog.

"You have a pleasant evening yourselves," Gustav's voice boomed out over the quiet conversation. "I'm going to stay here and escort my sister home and spend the night with her to make sure she's safe. Everything will be fine."

Rick stayed out of the way and let Bethany organize everyone. The two male cops shook Bethany's hand. The female detective gave her a hug and promised to come by so she could introduce her husband to really good food.

The three made it to the door and got tangled up with a late-night customer coming in.

Rick froze for a moment as Laurie entered, slipping carefully between the two men.

He tried to remember to breathe.

"Is it too late for coffee?" Laurie asked as the female cop waved and let the front door swing close. The cops headed down 22nd and disappeared from sight.

Bethany turned to Gwen and Tonio with a grand, warm smile. She did that so well.

"You two can head home and get some sleep," Bethany said. "We'll take care of everything. See you tomorrow."

Tonoi was gone like a shot. Gwen gave everyone a hug before she headed out. Probably had a gig she was playing later tonight, somewhere down in Fremont. It was Tuesday.

Bethany waited until it was just the four of them. Gustav appeared a touch nervous as he flipped *Flotsam's* door sign to Closed, but he was in complete control.

Rick could barely contain himself.

"That depends, young lady," Bethany finally replied. "Are you planning to be around for a while?"

Laurie fixed Bethany with a tight, pained look.

"As long as he'll have me," she whispered.

"Then you are always welcome," Bethany replied as she engulfed the tiny woman in a hug.

About the Author

Blaze Ward writes science fiction in the *Alexandria Station* universe as well as *The Collective*. He also write fantasy stories with several characters and series, from an alternate Rome to epic high fantasy in the desert. You can find out more at his website www.blazeward.com, as well as Facebook, Goodreads, and other places.

Blaze's works are available as ebooks, paper, and audio, and can be found at a variety of online vendors (Kobo, Amazon, and others). His newsletter comes out quarterly, and you can also follow his blog on his website. He really enjoys interacting with fans, and looks forward to any and all questions—even ones about his books!

Never miss a release!

If you'd like to be notified of new releases, sign up for my newsletter.

I only send out newsletters once a quarter, will never spam you, or use your email for nefarious purposes. You can also unsubscribe at any time.
http://www.blazeward.com/newsletter/

Reviews

It's true. Reviews help me sell more books. If you've enjoyed this story, please consider leaving a review of it on your favorite site.

About Knotted Road Press

Knotted Road Press fiction specializes in dynamic writing set in mysterious, exotic locations.

Knotted Road Press non-fiction publishes autobiographies, business books, cookbooks, and how-to books with unique voices.

Knotted Road Press creates DRM-free ebooks as well as high-quality print books for readers around the world.

With authors in a variety of genres including literary, poetry, mystery, fantasy, and science fiction, Knotted Road Press has something for everyone.

Knotted Road Press
www.KnottedRoadPress.com

Javier sometimes enjoys being a pirate, but he never forgets they made him a slave.

Join him in his adventures with the pirate ship *Storm Gauntlet*.

Part of the *Alexandria Station* universe.

Available at your favorite retailers.

Jessica could win the war, if they'd only let her...

Jessica Keller has a reputation as a maverick commander. It almost got her court martialed. Now it has gotten her a new command in an obscure sector, with orders to ignite a new front in the eternal war.

But her old nemesis, Imperial Admiral Emmerich Wachturm, stands in her way.

Worlds will fall before their feud ends, but only if she can forge her crew of strangers into a weapon. Otherwise, disaster looms.

Part of the *Alexandria Station* universe.

Available at your favorite retailers.